MOUNTAIN

MEN TRIPLETS

A Reverse Harem Secret Baby Romance

Rebel Bloom

CONTENTS

Chapter One

"Are we pretending that we're not going to end the night fucking in the bathroom like a couple of dogs in heat?"

My breath caught in my throat. The vulgar man sitting next to me at the bar shouldn't have turned me on the way he did. The fact that he did was proof that I hadn't grown up any. Not really. I was still turned on by the bad boys. "You clearly think highly of yourself."

"I just know what I want. Would you rather I offered to buy you dinner and pretend like I'd ever like bringing you flowers?" Julian, the name he'd given me when he sat down next to me at the bar, leaned in and whispered. "We both know what this is."

Damn him, but he was right. The moment he'd introduced himself, I'd known what he wanted and what I wanted, too. Dirty sex in a bathroom stall at a shitty bar fit the bill, but I was supposed to be waiting on my sister to show up for drinks. I'd had a long day breaking things off with a nasty ex, and I was supposed to be swearing off assholes. Yet, there I was, sitting next to a man I was one thousand percent sure was a giant asshole, thinking of all the ways I wanted him to make me come.

"Well, Cammie? What's your answer?"

That wasn't my name. The fact that I'd given him a fake name was evidence enough that I'd known what I wanted from him right away. Jesus, I was a monster to myself. Turning to face him, I let my knees brush against his thigh. "Do I look like the kind of woman you take into a bar bathroom?"

He grinned. "I mean..."

"Fuck you." I found myself grinning back at him. "Not here. My sister's showing up, and I want you gone when she gets here."

He growled, standing up to his full height. "Come on, Red. Lucky for us, I drove my truck here tonight."

I stood up and took the hand he offered. Ignoring the wave of warmth that came from his grasp, I followed him out of the bar, into the cold night air. It should've given me pause. It should've made me think twice about following the wild-looking man to the back edge of the parking lot. Instead, I just walked faster in my heeled boots.

Half an hour of flirting with him at the bar had been about ten times more foreplay than I'd had that year. Or maybe decade, even. I was so turned on by him that nothing else seemed to matter. Not the dirt coating his old truck, or the fact that he didn't open my door for me. I let myself in on the passenger side and held my breath as he started the truck and drove around to the back of the bar.

In the dark, with the heater rattling, Julian looked slightly terrifying. He was so damn big that the truck shrank away around him. Broad shoulders, thick chest and thighs, he was a man who clearly worked for a living. His rough hands called to my skin. I wanted him to manhandle me and make me forget everything else. I turned to face him, taking in the thick beard and too-long hair that kept falling into his eyes. He'd absently shove it off his forehead every time, something I doubted he even realized he did so often. Pale blue eyes practically glowed at me from across the truck.

My heart kicked up a gear, and my breath came faster. "Well?"

He laughed lightly and reached out to grab me. Like I weighed nothing, he dragged me into his lap. My ass hit the horn, but it was hard to focus on anything else but the way my thighs stretched around his legs.

"You know how dangerous it is for a little thing like yourself to just get into a truck with a man like me?"

I braced my hands on his strong shoulders and scowled down at him. "Do you know how dangerous it is for a man like yourself to just let anyone in your truck like this?"

He rested his hands on my hips and his fingers flexed, lightly squeezed me. "I think I'd be safe against you."

"Cocky asshole." I gently pressed my palm over his throat. "Is this the part where you lecture me about my choices? Or is this the part where you fuck me?"

Growling, he leaned into my hand, into me. "I can do both."

I lost my witty reply as he captured my mouth in a fierce kiss. The promise of it had been between us since he'd sat down next to me at the bar, but the real thing was so much better. He kissed like it was a lost art and he was doing his part to bring it back. His lips moved over mine, his tongue stroked mine, and his whiskey-tipped breath washed over my face as he inched back and stared into my eyes.

My stomach fluttered as a moment of tension passed between us. He looked at me with his brows furrowed, his eyes narrowed like I'd done something wrong. The kiss. It was too familiar, too good. It had no business being so connecting when it was a first kiss between strangers passing in the night.

"Shit." Julian grabbed my head and pulled me back into him. Hot and hard, he kissed me until I forgot everything I'd ever known about men. Had I ever even been kissed before?

I had two handfuls of his soft T-shirt without thinking, holding him close, desperation flooding through my body. My knuckles dug into his hard chest, but he just dragged me even closer. His massive hands in my hair tangled and tugged, the sharp bite of pain doing nothing to dull my desire. I kissed him hungrily, eager to taste the whiskey and mint on his tongue. For a second, I wondered if I was getting drunk on him.

My ass set the horn off again, but if Julian noticed, he didn't care. He kissed down my neck and sucked the tender spot just below my ear, marking my skin like he owned me. Even as I moved my hands to his hair to pull his head away, he chuckled darkly.

"Don't mark me. You don't own me."

"Sure as fuck looks like I do for the moment." With skill that should've been illegal, he leaned me back against the steering wheel and caught the button of my pants, popping it open with ease. "You're sassy. I like it."

I gasped as he slipped his hands into my jeans and cupped me through my panties. My breath caught in my throat, and I felt my core flood for him.

"Jesus, you're so hot, Red." Pulling me back into his chest, forcing my core even tighter against his hand, he kissed me again. Full of heat and desire, he devoured me. His beard was rough against my face, but I liked the scratch.

I arched my back and rocked my hips against him. With a jolting pleasure, Julian slipped his fingers inside my panties and thrust two of his thick digits into me. Crying out into his mouth, I grabbed his head and tangled my fingers in his hair. Full of him, I couldn't help working my hips up and down. I took my pleasure even as he gave it.

"That's it, baby, ride my fingers." Voice husky with desire, he worked my shirt up with his other hand. Seeing the lace bra under my t-shirt, he swore and rolled his thumb over my clit, causing me to jerk. "Do the panties match?"

I met his heated gaze with a lust-hazed one of my own. "Want to find out?"

Pulling his fingers out of me, he brought them up to his mouth and sucked them clean with a hungry growl. "Fuck me. Jesus, I knew you'd be sweet as pie the moment I saw you from across the bar."

I let out a surprised yelp as he pushed me off of his lap and kicked open the truck door. He was out in a flash and grabbing my ankle, pulling me across the truck bench until my legs were outside the truck and my ass was barely hanging on to the seat.

Julian tugged my pants down my legs and yanked them over my boots, revealing my plain cotton panties that definitely didn't match my bra. He grinned up at me and then tugged them off, too. He shoved them in his pocket and winked at me before stepping between my thighs and brushing his denim-clad erection against my bare core. "You're drenched, Red."

I spread my legs wider for him and fought any shyness as he looked me over. "Enough foreplay. I want you in me."

He reached over his head and pulled his t-shirt off, tossing it into the truck behind me. "What's the magic word?"

My mind went blank as I took in all the ink and muscle he was revealing. Muscles on muscles on muscles. And ink. So much black ink that decorated his skin and drew vivid images of who he was. I sat up and ran my hand over his chest, watching as his muscles flexed under my touch.

"Cammie."

I blinked up at him, lost in the story on his chest for a moment.

"You want to stare at them all night, or would you like to be fucked now?"

Snapping back to myself, I snarled at him. "I can do both."

He chuckled and shifted back enough to slip his fingers into me again. His thumb lazily circled my clit as he worked his thick digits in and out of me. "You have the hottest pussy I've ever felt, Red. I can't wait to destroy it."

I sat up on my elbows and rolled my eyes, despite the pleasure rolling through my body. The motion pressed my breasts together and drew Julian's attention to them. "That's a lot of talk for a man who still hasn't pulled his pants down."

Pulling out of me and licking his fingers clean again, he leaned forward and yanked my bra down, freeing my breasts. Swearing, he cupped them in his hands and shook his head. "Should be illegal to cover these up."

I wrapped my legs around his waist and lifted my hips. "Fuck me, Julian."

He met my gaze, his serious. "Say please."

I pushed him away and moved my hand to my core. "I'll just do it myself."

He growled as he watched my fingers circle my clit. His hands went to his pants and he quickly freed the biggest cock I'd ever seen in real life. I froze and stared at him with wide eyes. Julian gripped himself and stroked while meeting my eyes. "Say please, Red."

I swallowed audibly and licked my lips. I wasn't sure he wasn't right. He might destroy my body with that thing, but I was delirious with need after seeing it. Spreading my thighs open wider, I crooked my finger at him. "Come here."

He moved closer, that monster cock bumping against me. "You want this?"

I nodded.

"I want to fuck the shit out of you right now. I want to pound you into this seat so I'm driving around with your ass indention for months. I want to make you scream, but I'm not going to do any of it unless you open that pretty little mouth and say please."

I glared at him. My body was too far gone, but that didn't mean I was going to like giving in to him. I said the word he needed to hear like it was being chewed up with glass and spit out with gravel. "Please."

He surged forward and filled me without hesitation. In an instant, he was as deep in me as anyone had ever, ever been, and he was stretching me to the point just before pain. His answering groan and death grip on my thighs told me that he was just as affected as I was.

I caught my breath and dropped my head back on the seat. "Jesus."

Julian pulled out, not giving me a chance to get used to his size, and then slammed back into me. The pleasure and pain mixed into something I'd never felt before and my eyes rolled back in my head as he started a brutal pace of fucking me hard and fast.

"Look at me, Red. Look at me fucking you. You're going to remember me." His voice barely more than a growl, he leaned over me and caught my chin in his hand. He held my face and sent me a wicked grin when I met his eyes. "Now look how fucking perfect my cock looks fucking into your sweet little pussy."

I looked lower and swooned at the vulgar sight of his thick and angry-looking cock drilling into my body. It was shiny with all of my juices, and each time he pulled out, my lower lips looked like they were being pulled away with him. My body tried to suck him back in each time, and it was like watching the best porn I'd ever seen.

Instantly, my body spasmed around him. My core tightened and squeezed around him as a massive orgasm pummeled through me. I saw stars as everything in me broke for a moment of mourning over any orgasm I'd ever thought had been good before. My breath froze in my chest; my muscles were tight lines that pleasure was balancing on. And then Julian leaned down and whispered something so filthy in my ear that everything broke. Like a failed dam, it all came rushing out. White-hot pleasure coursed through me, twisting me and turning me until I wasn't sure if there'd ever be anything left of me.

Julian growled so loud I should've been worried about alarming the bar patrons, but then he was slamming into me with even more force and filling me with hot seed that I felt coat my walls and cervix, he was so deep. He plundered my body, his hands on my thighs punishing.

And just like that, I knew I was ruined for other men. It took one tryst with the man who told me his name was Julian, which lasted for less than twenty minutes, but I knew it. As much as he knew it. No one would ever be able to make me come like him.

As we came down from that wild high, Julian stumbled away, his back rigid. I wasted no time in dressing and slipping away. I hurried back into the bar and spotted my sister sitting at the bar before I could go to the bathroom to get cleaned up. So, I sat next to her and tried to pretend like I didn't have a stranger's come in me. I tried to pretend like I wasn't freaking out because the sex was too good and the connection had been too real. Never mind the fact that I wasn't on birth control.

When my sister went to the bathroom, I readjusted myself and gave myself a stern lecture. That's why I had to stay away from bad boys. I was an idiot for them. I made bad decisions and acted like a fool. I needed to get back to the city as soon as possible. I'd just put my head down and work, forgetting everything else.

Especially forgetting the man who'd fucked me stupid in the parking lot. Especially forgetting the way he'd whispered that I'd be fun to share, like he had a fucking clear view into my deepest, darkest fantasies.

CHAPTER TWO

One year and Nine Months Later

Briar's Point, Wyoming. The place that I'd come to know as Ground Zero. I navigated my car past the sign that declared the population of three thousand people and sighed. Highway 20 turned into Main Street for a couple of miles and led the stray passerby through the minuscule downtown area. A bar, a diner, a grocery store, and a few other miscellaneous businesses shined their windows regularly to draw people in. The bar was the true Ground Zero, and I made sure to avert my gaze from that back parking lot.

There were several people walking around town, curious gazes finding their way to me when they noticed the car wasn't one they were used to seeing. I had the same teeth-bared reaction that I would've in the city, a protective reaction to strangers looking in on Hank and me. Then I stopped myself and forced myself to smile. I wasn't in the city. I was in my sister's town, and I wasn't alone.

A stooped older man raised his hand in a wave and smiled brightly back at me. I waved back and drove on through. Hank gurgled from the back seat, his mouth preoccupied with the teether that had been ice cold when we left our hotel that morning.

"We're almost to Aunt Kara's, Hank. Then, we'll get out and stretch our legs." I reached back and lightly brushed my finger over the top of his head, feeling his silk soft hair. "You'd better get ready for Aunt Kara to spoil you, little man. She's got an entire party planned for you. You're going to be the belle of the ball."

Another gurgle of happiness came from him and a real smile stretched my lips. Hank was the happiest baby I'd ever known, and he gave all that happiness to me constantly. He saw me as his whole world, and after a year, I was still getting used to that. I didn't think I'd ever feel special enough to be that important to such an amazing little baby.

I turned off Main street and onto Malvern. Passing homes that had been built in the last two decades, I kept driving into the part of the neighborhood that had existed for nearly seventy years. The homes were spaced farther apart and slightly larger than the newer ones. There were a few mid-century homes and several ranch styles. At the very end of the street, Kara lived in a large brick house that had once housed the mayor of Briar's Point. She'd gotten it as a foreclosure ten years earlier when her husband, Tyler, got moved locally for work.

I'd always loved her house. The outside was so impressive and stunning, with love and care poured into every part of it. The inside was just as looked after, but there was something about the outside, with Tyler's ranging flowerbeds and Kara's hand-crafted windchimes, that made it feel magical.

I parked behind Tyler's truck with the silly little peeing on Chevy sticker on the back glass and gladly got out to stretch my legs and pull Hank out. Holding him in my arms, I bounced him gently and pressed a kiss to his nose.

"Hey, big boy. You ready to see Aunt Kara?"

"Aunt Mal!" Shrieking came from the front of the house and I turned just in time to see Casey shove her brother out of the way to run out of the house to me.

Taylor scowled at his sister's back and took off running after her. He was intent on retribution until I whistled to get his attention. "Aunt Mal! You're here!"

Casey slammed into my legs, quickly followed by Taylor. I grunted as I stumbled back a step and bumped into the car. "Whoa, careful. Don't forget Hank is breakable."

Taylor, the older of the twins by three minutes, crossed his arms over his chest and nodded. "Yeah, Casey, be careful."

Casey shoved her brother again and took off running, screaming at me the entire time. "Mom is waiting for you inside!"

I looked down at Hank and gave a quiet whistle. "Do you think you'll be a rowdy ten-year-old, too? Is that something I have to look forward to?"

I followed the sound of Casey and Taylor screaming at each other into the house and found a tired-looking Kara in the kitchen, pointing her finger at her kids and talking to them in a hushed tone. Both twins were angrily shouting that the other had started their fight, but Kara was having none of it. With a practiced glare, she silenced them both and sent them to their rooms to get ready for dinner.

"They get louder each time I see them. I wonder if it ever stops or if they just eventually become known as the world's loudest twins?"

Kara sighed and leaned against the island for a second before taking a deep breath and straightening. "Come here. I've missed you."

I walked into her open arms and gave her a one-armed hug while breathing in her familiar scent. I'd just seen her two months earlier, but I'd missed her, too. Ten years older than me, Kara had often been a mom to me more than a sister. Her Clinique perfume was as comforting to me as anything I'd ever found.

Pressing a kiss to my cheek, she cupped my face gently and smiled before turning her love on Hank. "Give him to me. Look at these cheeks!"

I passed him along and watched happily as she smothered him in kisses, and he ate it up. He loved her about as much as he loved me. Seeing her never failed to make him grin and try to talk to her. So far, he'd only said mama, but if Kara had her way, Auntie would be next.

"How was the drive?"

I grunted. "Long. I'm glad to be here."

Holding Hank to her chest while she moved around the kitchen, grabbing things, Kara barely contained her excitement. "We could barely contain ourselves. The twins have been extra wild in preparation for their favorite aunt."

"Only aunt."

"Tyler has been getting his poker chips shined, I swear." She put a plate with cheese and crackers in front of me and smiled. "And I have been counting the minutes. I'm so glad you're here, Mallory."

A wave of emotion hit me and I shoved a slice of cheese into my mouth to keep myself from breaking into tears. I was saved from myself when Tyler walked into the kitchen and spotted me.

"I thought I heard chaos arriving!" Holding his arms out, he pulled me into his big body and hugged me tight. "My favorite sister-in-law!"

"Only sister-in-law." I laughed and hugged him back, taking almost as much peace from his hug as I did from Kara's. "You feel healthy."

"Is that a fat joke?"

I rolled my eyes. "It's a comment on the fact that the last time I hugged you, you were skin and bones."

Kara passed Hank to her husband and stared up at him. "You saw him six months ago, right after treatment ended. He's doing so much better."

Tyler blew a raspberry on Hank's cheek, sending Hank into a fit of giggles, before cutting an annoyed look at my sister. "You two. When you're together, you talk about me like I'm not here."

Kara rolled her eyes, too, something we both did too much, according to Tyler. "He's gotten his crankiness back, too."

I grinned. "At least he still has his looks."

"Those he never lost." She wagged her brows at Tyler before laughing and wrapping her arms around his waist. "Sorry, honey. You're just too easy."

"That's what all those boys used to say about you, but that didn't stop me from falling in love."

I laughed a deep belly laugh that startled Hank. His lower lip turned down and his eyes welled up with tears that broke my heart. "Oh, I'm sorry, baby. Uncle Ty just made mommy laugh. Come here."

Kara smacked Tyler's chest playfully after I took Hank and pointed at him. "You're in trouble, mister."

"I'd better make myself useful before she actually gets mad at me. Can I start unloading the car?"

I frowned. "I can get it, Ty. You don't need to do that."

He frowned right back at me. "I'm fine, I can lift a few bags."

"Let him. If you don't, he'll spend the rest of the night lifting heavy things to prove a point." Kara waited until Tyler was gone with my keys to look at me and shrug. "He really is doing so much better. He'll wear himself out and spend the rest of the day in bed, pretending he's fine, if I'm not watchful of him, though."

I tried to hand Hank off to her, but she shook her head. "Kara, let me go help him."

"No, you've been driving all day. I'll help him bring your stuff in and you go check on my kids. Make sure they're not killing each other."

"Fine, but neither of you do too much. I can carry all of my crap in later. Alone."

She waved me off and vanished out the front door. I sighed and went in search of the twins to make sure no blood had been shed.

I found them in their playroom, fighting over a game. Instead of saying anything, I just walked in and sat in their hanging egg chair.

Casey stopped arguing and stared over at me. "Aunt Mal?"

I cradled Hank to my chest and raised my eyebrows. "You done fighting?"

Taylor walked over and ran his hand over the braided rope that held the chair in the air. "Are you going to stay for a while?"

I shrugged. "I don't know yet. Is it okay with you two if I'm here?"

Casey laughed. "Yes! We don't want you to leave."

"Mom needs you here." Taylor suddenly looked twenty years older. "She's been sad."

Casey elbowed her brother. "You're not supposed to tell people that."

I reached out and stroked both of their cheeks. "I'm not people. I'm your aunt. And your mom has had a lot going on. But I'm here now. I'll help with whatever she needs."

"Is Daddy dying?" Casey's big blue eyes welled up with tears that she didn't let fall.

Taylor hit her in the arm and scowled. "Don't even say that."

"You asked me!"

"Yeah, well, that's different."

"Enough, you two. Your dad isn't dying. He was sick, but he's getting better." I stood up and switched Hank to my other arm. "If the two of you can get along for more than ten minutes, I have something for you in the car. From the city."

"From the candy shop?" Taylor was instantly ten again. "Say it's from the candy shop!"

I laughed and nodded. "First one to the car is a rotten egg."

Casey took off at a sprint and then yelled. "Hey!"

Taylor crept forward dramatically. "I've never been a rotten egg!"

I passed both of them on the way down to the car, happy to have stopped the charging through the house for a moment, at least.

Chapter Three

Murder. That's what I was going to commit. My sister was as good as dead when I got my hands on her. I couldn't believe the gumption of her. The nerve!

Tyler looked up from his paper and winced. "Don't shoot the messenger."

I scowled. "I'm going to shoot your wife, and then I'm going to bring her back just to do it again."

Hank screamed at me from his highchair and reached desperately for more of his breakfast. I jumped into action and airplaned another bite of his food into his hungry little mouth.

"The party is ridiculous enough. Hank is just turning one. He's never going to know any of this happened. But the setup! It's my second day here. What is she thinking?"

"That you're a little high strung and could use a good lay?"

I scoffed at Tyler and then laughed. "I hate you."

He grinned. "You know Kara never means any harm. She's worried about you and how alone you've been. You know she just wants the best for you."

I puffed out a big breath and shook my head. "I've been alone by design. I don't need to be set up. I don't need a good lay. I had a good lay once, and it got me this beautiful little boy that I'd never regret, but he's enough."

"I've been meaning to talk to you about that." Tyler straightened his paper and put it aside. "So. The birds and the bees."

"Go to hell."

"Condoms, Mallory. Use condoms and you can have all the good sex you want to have without worry."

I fought another laugh. "I really don't like you."

"You love me. And you love your sister. Which is why you're going to meet the mystery man tonight and pretend to have a wonderful time. Because you don't want your sister to have one more thing to worry about. Right?"

"Hey, that's emotional blackmail, I'm pretty sure."

"Well, I never claimed to be good. I'm not above getting dirty to make sure my stressed-out wife relaxes for even one second." In an uncommon moment, Tyler grew serious. "Lord knows I've caused her enough stress for a lifetime."

I fed Hank another spoonful and sat in the silence for a moment, wondering what to say to Tyler to make him realize that Kara would've lived through a thousand times the stress of him being sick if it meant she got to love him for a second more.

As usual, though, Tyler didn't let the moment stay pensive for more than a second. "Anyway, I've seen Isaac. He's a fucking fox."

Taylor happened to be coming into the kitchen just as his dad swore. "Dad said a bad word!"

Casey appeared like magic. "Ten bucks to the swear jar, or eight to us. You choose."

I gaped. "Are you shaking down your dad?"

Tyler pulled out his wallet and pretended to be angry. "I'm raising a bunch of crooks if you ask me. Real mobsters. Here. Take my last few dollars and go."

I watched as they grabbed the money and ran, already discussing what they were going to buy. "Well, that was fun."

"I saved two dollars, to be fair."

"Is the swear jar a thing? Because I don't keep a lot of cash on me."

"Only if the twins hear you."

"So, yeah, it's a real thing." I sighed. "They hear everything."

"Try having sex in this house. It's damn near impossible." Tyler wagged his brows at me. "You could have sex in Isaac's house, though. No listening ears there."

"You're impossible!"

With a lot of grunting and swearing of her own, Kara came through the front door and made her way into the kitchen. She dropped an armful of grocery bags on the floor and looked up at me with her hands already raised as if I was pointing a gun at her. "I got your messages. I know you're pissy about Isaac, but it's fine. He's such a good guy, Mallory. And it's not like you have to marry him. I'm just asking that you talk to him."

I glared at Tyler and then sighed. "Fine. I'll talk to him."

"I'm serious, Mal. He's the nicest guy. And so handsome. He's—" She cut herself off. "Wait, what?"

"I said I'll talk to him. I'm not wearing that stupid dress you picked out for me, though. I'll look like a whale in it."

"We'll see about that."

"You know most people get a big win and then back off with the little battles."

"I just figure if I got you on the big battle, why wouldn't I try for the little ones?" She grabbed my face in her hands and leaned into me. "And don't you dare talk about yourself like that. You're beautiful."

Groaning, I focused on feeding Hank and trying to brace myself for what was sure to be a long day. "Beautiful enough to convince you to calm this thing down?"

Kara snorted. "You know better than that."

By the time the party started, I was in the dress she'd picked out. My hair and makeup had to be done to match, of course, according to my sister, and heels were somehow going to make my ass look magnificent. For my one-year-old's birthday party. Fighting Kara about it all had been too overwhelming, so I'd just given in and then settled into a chair at the kitchen table with Tyler next to me while guests that I didn't know moved through the house.

That wasn't completely true, however. I recognized some of the women from seeing them around Kara's before. They were basically strangers, though. Still, they all brought Hank a gift and talked to me about how cute he was. Hank was swept into Kara's arms pretty much right away, and she carried him around the house like he was next in line for the throne.

Kids ran through the house at max speed, their screams piercing my ears and making my brain hurt. I looked over at Tyler and sighed. He was staring around his house with an expression of exhaustion clear on his face. He'd done too much in helping set up for the party.

"Sorry about your house."

He turned his head to me and snorted. "Sorry about your dress."

I sighed louder. Running my hand down the silky material, I tried not to imagine the way it clung to my curves. Since having Hank, I felt like there were curvier than they should've been. "Your wife is a pain in the ass."

"Your sister is."

I nodded. "Yeah."

"Should we sneak out to the shed and smoke like we used to?"

I laughed, a hundred different memories flooding my brain. Tyler had been in my life for so long that he was like a true brother. We'd spent so many nights getting high in the shed out back that it was almost tradition. That was before Hank, though. "Ugh. I'm a mom now."

"Moms get high. Just ask Kara." He leaned in and wagged his brows conspiratorially. "I have the medical grade shit. Cancer shit."

"You're a terrible influence."

"Does that mean yes?"

I patted his cheek and shook my head. "Unfortunately, I've turned into a boring square. I stick to the straight and narrow these days. No drinking, no drugs, no—"

"Sex."

"Fun." I rolled my eyes at him and fought the childish urge to give into him and race out to the shed. It hadn't been easy living like a nun since I'd found out I was pregnant with Hank, that was for sure.

Kara popped up at that moment with a giant smile on her face. "Mallory! He's here!"

I winced.

"Stop that! Fix your face and push up your boobs. You look great!" Kara, bouncing Hank against her hip, glanced over her shoulder and then broke out in a welcoming grin. "Isaac! You made it!"

I looked up, expecting to see anyone but who I saw. Julian. Or Isaac, I guess. My blood all rushed to my face as I took him in. He was just as tall and strong as I remembered. I'd convinced myself that I'd made him bigger in my head, but looking at him then, I knew I hadn't. He was just a massive man. His hair was longer and lighter, but those vibrant blue eyes were just as bright. Everything female in me fluttered, and I gripped the edge of the table, half ready to run and half ready to beg him for a repeat of before.

"Isaac, this is my little sister, Mallory. Mallory, this is Isaac. Isaac owns and operates a ranch on the other side of town." Kara raised her brows at me, letting me know I needed to say something.

I was frozen. Isaac wasn't looking at me like he remembered me. There was interest on his rugged face, but nothing else. Did he not remember me? I wasn't about to out myself to Kara as having slept with the man already, so I finally managed to force a smile to my lips. "Nice to meet you."

He twisted a cowboy hat in his big hands and sent me a slow smile that set my body on fire. A scar cut through his lips that I didn't remember being there before, but it'd been dark in the bar and his truck. "Nice to meet you, ma'am. I hope you're finding Briar's Point to your liking."

Tyler snorted. "I think it just got a little better for her."

I kicked him under the table and forced another pleasant smile to my beet-red face. I didn't know what to say. I wanted to crawl under the table and die. Isaac seemed completely calm and collected. Did he really not remember me? God, that was insulting.

"Mallory's been in Briar's Point before, just for vacations and things." Kara pretended to notice something in the distance and gasped. "Oh, Casey is grabbing Taylor. Come on, Tyler. We'd better go get them."

Tyler grunted. "Why do you need—"

"Tyler, come on." Kara grabbed his hand and pulled him up. "Isaac can keep Mallory company until you're back."

I wanted to scream at my sister, but before I could do anything, she handed Hank to me and waved goodbye like the fucking queen of England. I bit my tongue and cradled Hank into my chest. His weight calmed me until I realized that I was holding the man's son and Kara had just left me alone with him.

If he felt awkward at all, Isaac didn't show it. He took the seat Tyler had vacated and turned to face me. His knee brushed against my hip, but he just apologized and shifted the smallest fraction away. The warm scent of him filled my nose, and it was hard not to breathe in deeper. "Your son?"

I cringed. "Yes. Hank."

"He's a beautiful baby." Isaac pushed up his sleeves and laughed when Hank reached for him. "He's not a shy kid, huh?"

I couldn't take my eyes off of Isaac's forearms. They were tan and dusted in blond hair, but they were bare. No tattoos. I sucked in a sharp breath and looked up at his face, surprised to find him already watching me.

CHAPTER FOUR

"No tattoos?"

Isaac's lips quirked up and he shook his head. "Nope. None."

"But..."

"You've met my brother, Julian, I'm assuming." Isaac leaned forward in his chair and silently asked permission to take Hank, who was still reaching desperately for him. "Triplets."

"There are three of you?" I slumped back into my chair and took a second to get my bearings. So, Isaac wasn't Julian. Just his identical brother, minus the tattoos.

Laughing easily, Isaac let Hank grab his face with sticky fingers as he watched me. "There are three of us. It's a lot, I know."

He had no idea. I was sitting with him, wondering how long it would be before he figured out Hank was his son, watching Hank try to grab for his father, having what felt like a heart attack. Isaac wasn't Hank's father, though. He had no idea. I was safe.

"I assure you I'm the good triplet." The way his deep voice and slow drawl said it made it sound like he'd be anything but good.

My body reacted with fire to him but I did my best to ignore it. It was probably just confused and still thinking he was his brother. "If I've learned anything about siblings in my life, it's that there's never a good one."

Isaac settled Hank on his lap and watched as Hank grabbed his finger and held it. "I don't think I've held a kid in fifteen, twenty years. Is it supposed to make you this scared? He's so small."

"Pretty much. I spent the first three months of his life carrying him with two hands at all times." I reached over and stroked the top of Hank's head. "Kara carted the twins around basically by their toes. She wasn't scared of anything."

"From what I know of your sister, that checks out."

"Do you know her well? She didn't mention how she knows you."

"Mostly just from around town. I helped her rehome a stray chicken the kids found once." He grinned to himself. "And I've watched her rip grown men to shreds in city council meetings."

"Oh, god. Did I just move to a town where my family is already hated because my sister bullies the men around?"

"Maybe." He met my eyes, and one side of his lip lifted. "I wouldn't use my last name around town if I were you."

I frowned and tried to read his expression. When his mouth cracked open into a big smile, revealing pretty white teeth, I laughed. "Hey! You really had me worried for a second."

He winked at me and then groaned slightly when Hank shoved his finger into his mouth to teethe on it. Drool dripped down his hand, and he looked at me with a helpless expression on his face. "Do I just...let him chew on me?"

"Let me get his teether and a napkin for you." Hopping up, I ignored his protest at being left alone with Hank and grabbed Hank's teether from the freezer. Snagging a napkin on the way back, I settled in my seat again and leaned in. "Look! You didn't kill him while I was gone."

"Funny."

I took his hand and gently pulled it away from Hank while giving Hank his teether. "He's teething. He's been an angel through it, but he is a bit more wet than normal because of it."

Isaac watched me as I rested his hand on my thigh to dry it off. His big palm was warm, and his fingers flexed while he studied me. "I like your dress."

My breath caught, and I realized just how close I was to him, with his hand resting on my upper thigh like he'd done it a million times. It felt like he should do it a million more times; it was that nice. I licked my lips and moved back to my original position, letting his hand fall away. "Kara. She doesn't just bully the townsfolk around."

"Well. She's usually right." His eyes flicked down to my mouth and then to Hank. "So, you married?"

I laughed. "No."

"Dating?"

My laughter died down quickly. Was he really asking for the reason I thought he was? "Single."

"Opposed to dating?" He turned back to me, and those pale blue eyes held my gaze with a heat I wasn't prepared for. I saw then that they were infinitely different from what I remembered of his brother's. The same beautiful shade of blue, but there was a depth to them that I hadn't seen in Julian's.

I felt awareness prickle my nipples and heat fill my core, something that hadn't happened in a long while. I bit my bottom lip and looked around the kitchen, realizing for the first time that we weren't alone. There were people sitting opposite us at the kitchen table. People moved around us, interacting with each other and having a good time.

I looked back at Isaac and found myself smiling. He hadn't bothered filling in the gaps my silence left in the conversation, and something about that radiated confidence that I couldn't help finding attractive. "It's not easy to date with a baby."

"I'm sure Kara would happily babysit." His grin cut through his full beard and his eyes lit up with laughter. "Or have you tried double dating?"

I laughed while rolling my eyes. "I haven't actually tried dating at all since I had him. Since I found out I was pregnant, actually."

"Not because I have any interest, at all, even in the slightest, but I think you really should go on a date with someone." He met my eyes again, heat clear in his gaze. "I wouldn't wait. I'd just grab the first guy you see, like right now, and tell him he's taking you on a date."

My heart thumped faster in my chest and I pretended to look away from him. "The first guy I see?"

Isaac surprised me by reaching over and cupping my chin in his big hand, just to pull my face back around to him. "Just any old guy you see first."

"Did my sister put you up to this?" I felt wary suddenly and unable to believe that he'd actually be interested. I felt out of shape and...motherly. How could I feel sexy when I just felt motherly nonstop?

"Your sister invited me to a baby's birthday party and told me that you desperately needed to be taken out, but I had no intention of doing anything other than being a gentleman and saying hello until I saw you." His thumb stroked the bottom edge of my mouth before he dropped his hand and smiled. "I'm a big boy, though. Say no and I'll accept it."

I fanned myself and looked around the room again, unsure of what the hell was actually happening. I spotted Kara peeking out from behind a couple of her friends, spying on us. "I hate my sister."

"I wasn't sure about her until tonight. Now, I think I really like her." Isaac caught Hank's teether as he tossed it and gave it back to him. "Looks like little man has quite the arm."

My hormones raged at seeing Isaac interacting with Hank and I felt myself slipping. Any promise I'd made to remain celibate and single crashed around Isaac's massive feet, and I turned to him fully, knees pressing into his leg. "You're taking me on a date."

"Want to go now?"

I stammered, not expecting him to mean right away. I thought there'd be some back and forth and then he'd take my number and call me in a few days. "Now?"

Kara popped up out of nowhere and took Hank. "I was missing this little nugget. Couldn't help overhearing that there's been a date proposed. You go on, Mal. I've got Hank. I'll even keep him in my room tonight in case you get home late."

My face flamed and I glared at her. "Kara, that's *so* nice of you."

She beamed at me. "Isn't it? You kids have fun, okay? Stay out as late as you want. Paint the town red."

Isaac looked over at me and raised his brows. "If red's not your color, we could try something else."

I fought a grin and shrugged. "Fine. I guess we're going out to paint the town some undecided color."

Tyler showed up, all wagging eyebrows and finger guns. "You remember the condom conversation, right?"

I stood up and flipped him off. "You suck."

Isaac followed me up and rested his hand on my lower back. "Thanks for inviting me. It was the best birthday party for a one-year-old I've ever been to."

"Do you like waffles, Isaac?" Tyler ignored my look and smiled. "We always have a big breakfast on Sundays. Waffles, bacon, real maple syrup, the whole nine yards. Come on over in the morning if you want. Around ten."

Kara nodded emphatically while simultaneously readjusting Hank and his teether. "Oh, yeah. Definitely come in the morning."

"Sure, if Mallory decides she can stand my company for a bit longer."

I pulled Hank into my arms and hugged him close. Kissing the top of his head, I told him I loved him and that I'd be back. I had a moment of grief at the idea of leaving him, but it was easier when I knew he was going to be with Kara. I handed him back to her and planted one last kiss on his cheek before pulling away.

Isaac's hand on my back moved up slightly as he leaned closer to me. "We can stay here. Or take him with us. I don't mind."

I shook my head and gave Hank one more kiss before I met Kara's giddy gaze. "I don't like you. Just so we're clear."

"No, you love me. Get out of here."

I stuck my tongue out at her and then looked way up at Isaac. "I just need to grab my purse."

I met him at the base of the stairs a few minutes later, after checking my hair and makeup in the bathroom, and then he led me outside to his truck. I had a moment of shame as he opened the truck door for me, knowing what I'd done with his brother in another truck. I felt guilty, knowing that he probably wouldn't want to take me out if he knew that I'd been with his brother.

"We really can stay here if you want to. I'm sure leaving Hank isn't easy."

Caught between the truck and Isaac, I looked up at him and shifted. "No, it's never easy. He's with his Aunt Kara, though, and she loves him almost as much as I do."

"What else is on your mind?"

I frowned. "Don't be so perceptive."

Laughing, he easily picked me up and set me in the truck. "So I should just ignore your looks of trepidation because I really want to take you out?"

"It's not trepidation. Not because of you, anyway." I sighed. "It's just... I know your brother."

Leaning into the truck, he put my seatbelt on and then stepped back, a smile on his face. "Most women know my brother, Mallory. That's not going to stop me from taking a beautiful woman out on a date if I want to."

"I *know* your brother."

"I said what I said." He saw my hesitance and leaned back in the truck. "If it bothers you, we don't have to do this. It doesn't bother me, though."

I raised my brows. "Is that not weird?"

"Only if you wish I were him instead of me."

"Not at all." I meant the words so thoroughly that I relaxed as soon as I said them. I knew that my attraction to Isaac had nothing to do with his brother and our short story, but it was all about Isaac. Maybe it was a mistake to go out with someone so closely linked to Hank's father, but no one knew. No one was ever going to know.

"Then I only have one question for you."

I waited.

"Would cooking for you at the ranch be off-limits?"

"At the ranch?"

"At my house, to be honest."

I hid a smile. "So, you weren't honest before when you said the ranch?"

"I was...not entirely." He leaned against the truck door and grabbed the top of the truck, exposing the strong line of his triceps through his shirt. "I had pure intentions, I promise."

"Fine. If you try to kill me, though, my sister will hunt you down." I shrugged as if I'd said the weather was nice. "Also, I watch a lot of true crime shows and I lived in the city for nearly a decade. I've taken plenty of self-defense classes."

"Noted. No killing, and watch my back because you're a master of defense." He backed away and inched the door shut. "How do you feel about burgers?"

"I feel strongly in favor of them."

"Burgers it is."

I watched him shut the door and walk around the truck, his eyes moving back to me even as he did. There was an attraction between us that felt good and exciting, but I was older and more mature after having Hank. I could control myself.

Isaac got in and started the truck. A slow country song played automatically and I blinked as I realized that maybe I shouldn't trust myself, after all. It'd been too long since I'd had an orgasm, and Isaac looked like he served up delicious ones. It was too late, though. I just had to hope that I wasn't that easy, that I'd give it up to a practical stranger on the first date. Not after I'd given it up to his brother as an actual stranger behind a bar.

Lord, help me.

CHAPTER FIVE

When Kara had said that Isaac owned a ranch on the other side of town, I had envisioned a ranch-style home on a few acres of land with a cow or two. I didn't know much about ranches, it seemed. What Isaac drove me to was something unlike anything I'd ever seen in person. I couldn't count the cows I saw; there were so many. There were what looked like miles of white fence, set against the backdrop of the mountains that surrounded Briar's Point. The ranch was also hidden away behind rows and rows of trees.

The ranch was like a magical land, tucked away in its own little green heaven. There was a huge barn, and then, down a long gravel driveway, a large house sat, welcoming and warm. White clapboard with a big, wraparound porch, it was something special to look at. I saw porch fans and a swing instantly and wanted to spend the night there, like in *Ya-Ya Sisterhood*. I wanted, instantly. Just wanted.

"My brothers and I were born and raised in this house. I had it redone as things came up, but a lot of it is still original to how my dad's dad had it. Like the porch swing." Isaac smiled at me and nodded. "Want to try it out?"

I nodded and hurried out of the truck. "It's amazing."

Leading me up to the swing, he sat on it with me, his arm stretched out along the back of it. "This thing has gotten a lot of use over the years."

"I'm sure. It's beautiful. And the breeze is amazing, too." I sighed and leaned back in the seat. "It feels a little like heaven."

"You can sit out here while I get the burgers ready to go on the grill if you want." He caught a strand of my hair and gently tugged it. "Or you can come in and look around. Whatever you want."

I laughed. "I have the run of the land, huh?"

"Yeah, I'm helpless against the powers of that dress. Pretty sure Kara got in my brain and stole that dress from my dreams. Remind me to thank her at breakfast tomorrow."

I groaned. "You don't have to come to that if you don't want to. They're just so busy playing matchmakers, on my second day in town, might I add, that they don't stop to think that maybe you have something better to do."

"I don't." With a lingering look and a shake of his head, he opened the front door and stepped into the house. "Come in if you want. I won't be long."

I sat on the porch for a few minutes longer, just enjoying the chilly evening breeze and looking out at the mountains and forest. The beauty of it all was almost enough to convince me that I was dreaming. The land, the house, the man, it was all an insane change from where I'd been just two days before.

All alone in the city, surrounded by buildings and people non-stop, never having a moment of peace. It was crazy how much a handful of hours could change everything. Men had been the farthest thing from my mind when I was alone with Hank. I was too worried about finding reliable childcare and getting home safe to him to ever bother thinking about dating.

There I was, though, just a couple of days later, on a date. Kara had really worked her magic. She hadn't started small and built her way up, either. Isaac was stunning to look at. He was perfectly my type with his sexy Grizzly Adams look. He also seemed nice, which hadn't been my type before Hank. Nice on Isaac was sexy, though.

I made my way into the house, taking in everything as I searched for the kitchen. The décor was manly with lots of leather and browns, but it was warm. There were books everywhere, stacked haphazardly all over the place, but it just added to the charm. I touched the spine of a few of them, not even dusty, and smiled when I noticed there were a few romances in the stacks.

"You're a romantic at heart, huh, Isaac?"

He poked his head out of the back room, and his cheeks darkened when he saw where I was looking. "I'm not going to lie to you twice in one day, so I have to own up to those, but that's all I'll say."

Laughing, I followed him into the kitchen and settled at a stool at the island to watch him form the burgers. He'd shed the flannel shirt he'd had on and was in a t-shirt that stretched across wide shoulders and strong arms. I had to force myself to stop staring.

"I have beer and water. I would've gotten something different, but I didn't plan on Kara being onto something when she pushed us together."

"Don't give her credit for this. She'll never shut up about it."

"I think that ship has already sailed. She looked very smug as we were leaving." Isaac paused. "She also shoved a condom into my hand while you were grabbing your purse."

I gasped. "No, she didn't."

"She did."

I covered my face with my hands and groaned. "She's dead to me."

"I wasn't sure what to say to her after I realized what she'd given me, so I just bumped fists with her and told her I wouldn't use it all in one place."

Surprised laughter bubbled out of me, and I snorted. Tears rolled down my cheeks as I thought about what Kara had made of that.

"I'm realizing now that I probably really concerned her." He tossed the condom onto the island and laughed. "Also, do you think she already had the Magnums on hand? Or did she go out shopping for this?"

I snorted again and crossed my legs as I laughed harder. "Stop! I'm going to pee myself!"

"Bathroom's behind you." He bit his lip as he watched me try to right myself before I stood up. "You're fucking beautiful when you laugh."

I scrunched up my nose and fought back a protest as I hurried into the bathroom. While I washed my hands after, I stared at myself in the mirror above the sink and shook my head. I didn't see what Isaac saw, but I liked that he seemed to like what he saw. I liked feeling desirable after so long.

Coming back out, I found Isaac chopping potatoes. He looked up at me and his eyes heated. A part of me, the part that hadn't been out in almost two years, wanted to hide in the bathroom. The rest of me wanted to know what all that heat entailed.

"This is a lot different from how I thought my night would go." I shrugged and sat down across from him. "Honestly, I've never really had good experiences with dating, so I'd kind of sworn off it after Hank came along. So, this is a little weird for me. Like, I can't stop the urge to tell you that I've peed on myself laughing two times since I had Hank and I'm concerned that it's going to happen again and it almost just did happen again. But that's a really embarrassing thing to say on a first date, right? So, why did I do that?"

He put the knife down, and I could see he was fighting a smile. "I don't think it's embarrassing. Embarrassing is going to a birthday party for a baby to get a date. I'm the one who should be awkward right now, not you."

"I got picked up at a birthday party for a baby, so really, I'm the awkward one." I groaned. "I got picked up at *my* baby's birthday party."

"So. For the record. I did pick you up." He puffed his chest out and stroked his beard. "Prettiest lady at the party, too."

I reached across to grab the cutting board and knife and pre-occupied myself with cutting potatoes even as I rolled my eyes at him. "I'm already here; you can stop complimenting me."

"I'm not complimenting you to get anything from you. I'm just stating what I see. And I like what I see, a lot." He shrugged like he wasn't saying anything big. "You're mincing the potatoes."

I looked down to realize I'd been cutting the same poor potato into tiny chunks. Dropping the knife, I cleared my throat and walked around the island to get to the sink to wash my hands. I was aware of Isaac behind me, and that awareness traveled down my spine in a tantalizing way.

Leaning against the counter next to me, he looked down at me and smiled. "I haven't had a date in a long time, either. I'm rusty, I'm sure. There's no pressure, though."

My stomach fluttered and I felt urges that I hadn't felt in too long. He was so attractive, and he was funny. I knew basically nothing about him, but there was no way I could get involved with him on a more serious level. Not with Julian potentially ever being in the picture. I couldn't date him. I could only enjoy him for that moment and then go back to my life of focusing on Hank.

"You're giving me an interesting look, Mallory." Isaac stood up straighter and moved closer to me. "What's on your mind?"

Even his ability to ask about my thoughts was sexy. The man was a complete package, from what I'd seen so far. I blew out a rough breath and turned to face him fully. "I don't date."

He grinned. "And yet here we are."

"I can't date you. I have Hank, and he's my focus. Plus, the thing with your brother. That would be weird later." Not to mention disastrous. "But I'm so attracted to you that I can feel it all the way down to my toes."

Quirking an eyebrow, he absently rubbed his hand over his flat stomach. "So?"

"So, if...if you were interested in one night, tonight, then that would be okay." I would spend a lot of time later thinking about my morals, but I felt like a guitar string pulled too tight. Something was going to snap. Being around a man I found devastatingly good-looking for the first time in so long and hearing him tell me he found me attractive, it was like setting off a bomb in my brain. A one-night stand, something I'd sworn off, felt like the answer.

"Spell it out for me, Mallory."

I shivered at the gruff tone his voice had taken on. "Sex. Do you want to have sex with me tonight?"

He grabbed my hips and pulled me into his body, letting me feel the stirring that was happening south of his belt. "Yes. But I don't think I like your terms."

I couldn't think with his hard body pressing against mine. I let my arms dangle loosely at my sides, unsure if I should touch him. "No?"

"What if I'm greedy? What if I want more than one night?" He leaned into me and brushed his nose along my neck. "What then?"

I tipped my head to the side to expose more of my neck to him. He was so hot against my body, and his breath on my sensitive skin was giving me chills of pleasure "Only tonight."

"Tonight, and then you reevaluate your plans."

I smiled and finally lifted my hands to rest them on his shoulders. "Are you negotiating?"

"To get more of you, yes."

"You don't even know if you're going to like this. I could be terrible at sex. I could have a hairy nipple hiding under my dress that gives you nightmares for years."

"Reevaluate your plans after." He stroked his hand up my rib cage and his thumbs teased the skin just under my breasts. "Please."

I nodded, already too far gone. "Fine. After."

With that, he pulled away and grabbed another potato. "Will you grab that onion over there?"

I stumbled. "What?"

"I promised you dinner. I'm going to cook for you still."

I stupidly stood frozen, watching as he carried on like we hadn't just made plans to have sex. "But..."

With a grin at me over his shoulder, Isaac amped up my desire even higher. "If I only get one chance to convince you to see me again, I'm going to make it count. Now, can I have that onion?"

Chapter Six

We sat on the porch while Isaac grilled the burgers. I was pretty sure he was trying to seduce me with the swing, and I wasn't sure he wasn't onto something. We watched the sun dip below the mountains as the burgers cooked and then we sat in the darkness, gently rocking back and forth in silence for a bit. It was peaceful, and it was lulling me into a sense of safety.

"The city was never like this. It was never quiet."

"It wasn't what you wanted?"

"I think it used to be. After I had Hank, though, nothing felt safe there. I was alone, and I had to rely on people I didn't know well enough to watch Hank for me. I spent so much time worrying about where he was while I worked that I barely got anything done. I loved the city when I was younger. I moved there as soon as I turned twenty and never thought I'd leave."

"Things change, though." He stretched his arm out behind me, and I felt him playing with my hair. "There was a time when I didn't want this place or anything of the work that came with it."

"What changed for you?"

He went still for a beat and then sighed so silently that I might've missed it if I wasn't leaning closer to him. "Family. I realized that I don't want to let it slip away."

"Are you close with your family?"

"Some of us are closer than others. Every family has a history, and ours isn't all good. Some of us can't let go and move on." He stood and walked over to the grill. "Looks like these are done. You ready to eat?"

I watched his back as he worked the grill and fought the urge to wrap my arms around him. He had layers, and damn him, he was drawing me in. I sighed to myself and stood up. "Yeah. Food sounds good."

We ate at the counter and talked between bites, but as the food went away, so did our conversation. I couldn't stop thinking about what was coming, and the anticipation had me wiggling around in my seat. Every stolen glance had weight and heat to it; each clumsy bump of our knees felt like an electric shock.

With still half of my dinner left on my plate, I pushed it away and turned to Isaac. "This is killing me."

He paused with a fry halfway to his mouth and dropped it, turning to me completely. His eyes roamed my face, and then he brazenly looked over my body. His slow perusal just amplified my arousal. I wanted him to do something. The waiting was torture.

"Isaac..."

He licked his lips and then stood up and held his hand out to me. "Come on."

I wasn't sure where we were going, but I was pretty sure I would've walked off a cliff if he told me we'd have sex at the bottom. Out of the kitchen and down a hallway, he led me into a bedroom with a massive bed in the middle of it. The bed was made, more books stacked on each side of it, and the dark blue bedding looked soft. I wanted to know what it felt like under my naked back.

Isaac led me to the side of the bed and sat down in front of me. He pulled me between his legs and wrapped an arm around me. I braced my hands on his shoulders and bit my lip at the feeling of his muscles flexing under me. He was finally eye to eye with me and my breath caught at being so close to him.

He ran his hand up my arm and cupped my neck, his eyes falling to my mouth. Gently pulling me into him, he pressed his lips to mine, and the sound of pleasure he made vibrated from his chest and weakened my knees.

I leaned into him and felt my stomach tighten as his lips moved over mine. He kissed me gently, patiently, until I dug my fingers into his shoulders and made a pathetic whimper of need. I felt like I was coming unwound, almost two years of tension threatening to blow if he didn't kiss me harder and touch me everywhere.

Sensing what I needed, he stroked his tongue into my mouth and kissed me passionately. He held me tighter and caught the ends of my hair in his fist. His body consumed mine, his strength evident as he easily lifted my body onto his lap and held me there, even as he kissed me deeper. Draped over his thighs, my dress stretched and left my white panties exposed. I felt the cool air of the room brush over the damp spot that had formed in them, and then Isaac's erection pressed directly into me as he shifted me closer.

I moaned into his kiss and wrapped my arms around his neck. "Isaac..."

He dropped his hands to my thighs and pulled back from me enough to look at me. "Jesus, you're beautiful."

I blinked as I tried to calm down enough to appreciate the moment. "*You're* beautiful."

He grinned as he leaned in and reached around to grab the zipper at the back of my dress. "I've been dying to pull this thing down since I saw you."

I shivered as he worked the zipper down to my lower back and then pulled the dress forward on my shoulders. My heart pounded, and I tangled my hands in his hair, even as my body pulsed. "I'm not going to apologize for my body, but it isn't the same after having a baby."

Pulling the dress down my chest, exposing the thin white bra I wore, Isaac dropped his hands back to my thighs and squeezed. "There's nothing to apologize for. You're fucking stunning."

I held my breath as he slid his hand higher and, while watching me, stroked his finger over my panties. My hips tilted into his hand, and he rewarded me with another stroke. "It's been too long. I feel like my head is going to fly off."

Isaac kissed me again while pulling my panties aside and stroking his fingers through my wetness. His answering growl of pleasure reminded me of his brother, but I shut that thought down and let my head drop back. He kissed my neck and throat, biting my bra straps and pulling them down my shoulders while pushing his thick finger into me. I grabbed harder at his hair and moaned loudly, the feeling of him pushing into me both relieving and insanity making.

"Can you take one more?" Without waiting for my answer, he pulled his finger out of me and pushed two back in.

My core felt stretched and full, something I'd missed. I arched my hips, rocking over his fingers, and moaned his name again. "So good."

He scissored his fingers in me and then pushed my bra down with his other hand. Exposing my breasts to his hungry eyes, he swore and took turns cupping them and exploring what made me gasp. Lighting pinching my nipples got him the biggest response, so while he pulled his fingers out and then pushed three back in, he pinched just a breath harder and swallowed my desperate cry in a hot kiss.

It was all so much after not having anything for so long. I held my breath as the overwhelming sensations rocked over me, waiting for them to ease up. When they just grew stronger, I sucked in a ragged breath and begged him to make me come. I needed something, anything, to release the building pressure that was killing me.

"Ride my fingers, Mallory. Show me what you want." His voice was rough, the order clear, as he twisted his thumb so it brushed my clit with my every move. "Ride me until you come."

I bit my lip hard even as I lifted myself almost all the way off of his fingers and then dropped back down. He stretched me and filled me, the heat in his eyes shocking as he watched me. I braced myself on his shoulders and dropped my head back, feeling everything so much that I wasn't sure I'd survive an orgasm. Still, I lifted myself again and slid back onto his fingers. Again and again, until I was lost to my pleasure and taking what I needed. I rode his hand hard and fast while his other hand held my bouncing breasts steady enough for his mouth to find my nipples. His teeth found the line between pleasure and pain even as his thumb rolled over my clit when he could reach it.

Harder and faster, I rocked my hips against him, riding him without inhibitions until the first wave of pleasure slammed into me and I jerked. Feeling my orgasm hitting, Isaac locked his arm around my waist and held me down on his fingers while rubbing my clit furiously, drawing it all out. My orgasm grew bigger and my breath caught as it finally crested and a ragged cry ripped from my mouth. Wave after wave of pleasure washed over me and left me limp in his arms, my body still full of his fingers and my nipples almost bruised, brushing against his chest with every gasped breath.

"Fuck." Isaac pressed his lips to my head and held me tight. "You're a fucking firecracker, aren't you?"

Still gasping for breath, I moaned when he pulled his fingers out of me and stood up. I wrapped my legs around his waist and held on, even while feeling like I was too heavy to be held. "Put me down before you hurt yourself."

Turning us around and dropping me onto the bed, he looked down at my exposed body, panties askew and bra pulled down, and his eyes practically glowed with desire. Leaning down, he grabbed the sides of my panties and jerked them away from my core. The panties went flying, and then he was on his knees, burying his face between my thighs.

I cried out as he licked me up and down, drinking in my juices and simultaneously stroking my clit and then fucking me with his tongue. He licked my lips, my thighs, even down lower to the spot no one had ever touched like that. He devoured me, his growls of pleasure mixing with my cries until the room sounded as animalistic as I felt.

His hands reached up and cupped my breasts, stroking them and squeezing them. He lifted his head long enough to look at me with a shiny face and order me to lose the bra and dress. "Naked. I want you naked, now."

I stumbled through undressing while he lifted my hips to expose more of my core to his hungry mouth. I froze while he circled that forbidden bud with the tip of his tongue and then melted when he moved back to my clit and sucked hard. I was building towards another huge orgasm so fast after the first one that my body felt foreign to me. Drying to undress it while he did that was impossible.

Just when I thought I'd come again, he lifted his head, gave me a hot look, and pulled at my clothes, helping me. When I was naked, he seemed to realize that his clothes were all still on and he gave a frustrated grunt while standing and stripping.

I watched as his strong chest was exposed, tan and coated in a dusting of blond hair, then his thighs as he shoved his pants down. He kicked them off and then pushed his briefs down with as much care, suddenly standing naked in front of me. His cock was thick and long, the head a deep red with veins standing out all the way down it. I didn't know whether to worship it or run from it.

Gripping himself in his big hand, Isaac closed the gap between us and stroked his head over my lower lips. I was so wet that it slipped through my folds easily, and he bumped into my opening, a feeling so good that I almost lifted my hips to take more of him in.

"Condom." He seemed to be reminding himself.

I grabbed his hand when he tried to leave. "Clean. And on birth control. So much birth control after the last time. If you want…"

He swore and gripped my thighs in his hands, dragging my ass to the edge of the bed. "I think I'll marry you."

I laughed, but then he was pushing into me, stretching me. My hands gripped the bedding and my mouth fell open in a silent cry as he filled me. Inch by inch, until the tip of him rested against my cervix and his balls pressed into me. I felt my eyes cross and my world shift once again. "Oh, god, Isaac. Oh, god."

He leaned forward and wrapped his hands behind my neck, holding me locked onto his body, and then he slid almost all the way out of me before thrusting back in. His eyes found mine and he watched me as he did it again. Pulling out and then thrusting back into me, fucking me hard and slow. My body pulsed and twisted under him, needing more or less, or anything. I felt wild and feral with desire for him. Grabbing at his arms, I twisted my hips and swore his name.

"That's it, Mal. Take me." He thrust into me faster, his face just as feral as I felt. His muscles bunched and released under my hands and his hands tightened on the back of my neck as he held me still for him. He dropped his mouth to my nipples and gently tortured my body into submission to him. He had to know I was helpless against his desires and my own.

Harder and faster, he took me almost roughly until I was barely hanging onto my sanity once again. I cried out his name like a prayer and grasped for any hold I could get. I ended up with handfuls of his hair, pulling his head harder into my chest.

He shoved his hand between our bodies even as his thrusts sped up and lightly pinched my clit. Pleasure shot through my body like lightning, and another strong orgasm slammed through me. I shook and screamed out, my entire being feeling like it was shattering apart under him. Isaac's thrusts faltered, and he growled into my chest as the first shot of his seed flooded my core.

I came apart and crumbled under him, tears of pleasure leaking from the corners of my eyes as I went limp under him. My body, tired and sore, still milked his as he filled me with his come. I loved the feeling of it in me, the naughtiness of it. I loved knowing that I'd done that to him.

Isaac slowly lifted his head and straightened, his face a mask of pleasure and hunger still. He rested his hand on my stomach, stroking me, and gave me a slow grin that made my core flutter around his shaft. He swore and leaned back to gently pull out of me. Instead of moving away to clean himself up or let me get cleaned up, he stood there and rubbed his softening cock over my lips and thighs. He watched as our juices leaked out of me and then pushed his tip back into me. It was something so dirty and possessive that I shivered and flushed all over.

"You are fucking perfect." Voice still rough with desire, he looked up at me and shook his head. "Fucking better than perfect."

Completely open and exposed, I found myself melting to him and already readjusting my one-time-only stance. A man like Isaac definitely deserved two times. Or three.

CHAPTER SEVEN

I got back home in the middle of the night, sore and exhausted. I kissed Isaac goodbye, telling him that it couldn't happen again, even as he grinned and told me he'd see me later. What would've typically pissed me off just made me smile as I slipped inside and went to my room. I took a shower and washed Isaac off of me before going to grab Hank from Kara's room. I held him for a while before putting him down in his crib and falling into a deep sleep almost instantly.

Kara woke me up with the sun, shaking me and splashing me with water from the cup of hot water she insisted on drinking every morning. "Hey. Asshole, wake up. You scared the shit out of me. Haven't you ever heard of kidnapping? I thought someone had snatched Hank in the middle of the night when I woke up to find him missing."

I groggily sat up and rubbed my eyes. "Sorry. I just grabbed him when I got home. I didn't even think."

Silence met my apology, and I had to actually open my eyes and face the morning sun to see what had Kara speechless. I blinked about a hundred times before I could see her clearly, and then I wished I hadn't bothered. She was staring at me with a shit-eating grin on her face.

"You fucked Isaac!"

I slapped my hand over her mouth and looked at the bedroom door, fully expecting one of the twins to be there. "Oh, my god, Kara!"

She smacked my hand away and laughed. "You dirty lady, you really did! You fucked him, and you have the evidence all over you!"

I jumped out of bed and rushed into my connected bathroom to glare at my reflection. My sleep shirt was a worn and ragged old t-shirt that was cut to hang off my shoulder, and it revealed a lot of red, beard-burned skin on my neck and chest. My lips were still red and swollen from kissing Isaac like my life depended on it. There was a glow to my skin that I couldn't help but blush over. Isaac did good work.

I poked my head out of the bathroom and looked at my sister, grinning like an idiot on the end of my bed. "Okay, I did it, but I don't need any lip from you about it."

She laughed loudly, only belatedly realizing that Hank was still sleeping. "I am so proud of you! Isaac is so beautiful. God. What I'd do to be ten years younger and interesting in swinging."

Tyler appeared in my bedroom doorway and raised his eyebrows at his wife. "Really, Kara?"

She had the decency to look guilty. "I meant I'd be swinging with you, honey!"

He looked thoughtful for a second. "Let me pick our fourth and I'm in."

"No fucking way." Kara waved him away and looked back at me. "Tell me everything."

"No!" I tried to shut the door, but Kara spoke up before I could ignore her.

"Wait! I actually came to say I got you an interview tomorrow morning. The lumber yard in town needs someone in the offices right now. Their last lady is on maternity leave and Blake didn't get a replacement yet."

"Really? That's great!" I caught sight of my reflection again and winced. "I'm going to need to cover this all up before I go down and face the twins."

"Tell me about Isaac and I'll help."

I came out of the bathroom just to glare at her. "You're a perv; you know that?"

"Sure, but that's okay." She shrugged. "I'll just ask Isaac when he gets here for breakfast, I guess."

My eyes widened. "No. He can't come after last night!"

"Why? What the hell did you do to him?"

"I didn't do anything to him! We just did it." I lowered my voice. "A few times. And it was fucking amazing, but I told him it was a one-time thing. I can't have breakfast with him this morning! That's so awkward!"

"Why the hell would you tell him that it was a one-time thing?"

I gestured at Hank and then at myself. "We're a package deal, and I didn't come here to start dating."

Kara rolled her eyes dramatically and shook her finger at me. "You're going to eat your words. Isaac is a determined man."

"You think he really is going to show up?"

"Oh, yeah. Unless you tried to do some weird stuff with him last night." She giggled. "I once tried to touch Tyler's...you know. He didn't speak to me for a week."

Staring at my sister, I managed to keep a straight face for a few seconds before I lost it. Laughing, I shook my head. "Poor Tyler."

"Poor Tyler. I thought I was doing him a favor. Poor me. That's not a cute place on men." She stood up and put her hands on her hips. "Get ready. You've got an hour before breakfast. Expect company."

"Kara, I can't sit across the breakfast table from him after last night!"

"Don't sit across from him, then. Sit next to him." She strolled out, leaving me just as quickly as she'd joined me.

I sank onto the bed and groaned. Things were going to be awkward. I didn't love being in awkward situations. I tended to make a fool of myself. Maybe Isaac wouldn't show up, though. Maybe he'd forgotten all about breakfast in the commotion of the night.

I still found myself dressing with the chance of him showing up in mind. My good leggings and a flowy top that hinted at my cleavage but hid any of the extra baby weight I'd never been able to get rid of. My red hair, the same hair that Isaac had said he loved while wrapping it around his fist the night before, was up in a bun, and then I did enough makeup to hide any traces of our night together.

I even had time to get Hank up and bathe him. Dressing him in one of the adorable outfits Kara had for him, I carried him downstairs and got him set up in his highchair. Kara was manning the kitchen, making too much food. Tyler was sitting at the table again, a book in his hands.

"Did you remember our talk last night, young lady?"

I ignored him and talked to Kara while feeding a playful Hank. He splashed his food, making a mess of himself, but he was so happy about it that I couldn't be upset about it. "Do you have the strawberry syrup?"

"For our first breakfast with our future brother-in-law? You bet I do."

Tyler snorted. "Should've talked to me instead."

"Kara, that's not funny."

"I think it is." She waved a spatula at me. "I told Tyler your one-night crap."

"Have you seen Isaac?" Tyler scoffed. "You'd be crazy to walk away after one night."

Kara made an agreeing sound. "Everyone's seen Isaac."

The doorbell rang, and I glared at both of them while standing. "If either of you says anything weird over breakfast, I will out you as wannabe swingers."

Tyler moved over to take over with Hank. "If we're going to get him to swing with us, we're going to have to talk to him about it, Mallory."

"I hate you both."

Casey and Taylor chose that moment to walk in. Casey was still rubbing her eyes as she woke up. "Why do you hate Mom and Dad?"

Taylor grunted. "Probably because they made her wake up so early."

I opened the door and found myself blushing as I looked up at a fresh-looking Isaac. With his hair still wet and a knowing smile on his face, he was too sexy for it to be legal. I automatically leaned against the doorway, feeling a little swoony. "Hi."

He wrapped his arm around my waist and pulled me into his chest, quickly leaning down to deliver a hard kiss. "Hi."

"Mom! Aunt Mal is kissing Mr. Isaac!" Casey's shout jolted me away from Isaac.

"Leave your aunt and her new man friend alone!"

I covered my face with my hands and found something sticky on my forehead. Groaning, I realized I had Hank's breakfast on me. "Just run now, while you can."

Isaac shook his head. "Not a chance."

I pouted and walked back into the kitchen. "I'm disowning any of you who do anything embarrassing. That goes double for you, Casey."

Kara slapped me with her kitchen towel. "Come over here and wash the baby food off your face."

"Mr. Isaac, why were you kissing Aunt Mal? Are you her boyfriend?"

I glared at Kara. "Do something!"

"What do you know about boyfriends?" Tyler turned a stern look on his daughter and shook his head. "You know nothing of boyfriends until you're twenty-five. You hear me?"

"Dad, I've kissed a boy. I'm not a baby."

"You didn't kiss Ryan Miller, stupid. He was drowning and you tried to give him mouth-to-mouth."

"Ryan Miller drowned?" Kara looked shocked. "When did this happen?"

"No, he wasn't actually drowning. He was faking to trick Casey, and she fell for it." Taylor yawned. "Is breakfast ready?"

"You kissed a boy?" Tyler handed a messy Hank off to Isaac and shook his head at his daughter. "No, no, no. No kissing boys."

"What about Taylor? He can just kiss girls, but I can't kiss boys?" Casey crossed her arms over her chest and scowled at her father. "That's sexist."

"He can't kiss girls, either!" Tyler rubbed his head. "No one can kiss anyone. Except your mother and me. We can kiss."

"What about Aunt Mal and Mr. Isaac?"

Isaac bounced Hank on his leg and grunted. "I think we get to kiss, too."

"So, everyone gets to kiss except for us?" Casey let out an angry groan and stomped to the fridge and shoved her head inside. "This house can be so stupid sometimes! Where is my orange juice?"

I met Isaac's eyes over the commotion of Kara and Tyler trying to get Casey to stop being a teenager before she was even a pre-teen. He grinned and shrugged. I couldn't help grinning back.

Breakfast went like that. When it was finally over, I was almost giddy from all the looks I'd been sharing with Isaac, but I had a headache from listening to Casey and Taylor fight the entire time. Even Hank was starting to get fussy. His teeth were bothering him, and I'd left his teether out all night, so he didn't have the cold to soothe him.

I held him in my arms and rocked him, even as he cried and rubbed at his teeth. I felt terrible for him. Nothing I tried to give him made a difference, and he was in full-on wailing before too long. I winced and searched through the freezer for something he could chew on. When the only thing I could find was a bag of peas, I got desperate and gave him a corner of the bag to chew on while I said goodbye to Isaac, who was probably officially regretting coming over.

Holding Hank and the peas, I found Isaac standing on the front porch, a smile on his face. He looked me over and shook his head. "You have your hands full."

I nodded. "I'm surprised there's not a comical trail of dust following you out of here right now."

"Nah. This was fun. Reminds me of my house growing up." He leaned in and planted a kiss on my forehead. "I've got work to do on the ranch, and you're busy, but I'm not running. I'm coming back for another date soon."

"Why would you want that?"

He just smiled and shrugged. "See you later, Mal."

I watched him leave and looked down at Hank. "Maybe he's crazy. Why else would he be interested in us? We're kind of a mess."

As if on cue, Hank made a straining face and graced me with a foul smell. I sighed and tried to remember how I'd ever felt sexy the night before.

Chapter Eight

The next morning, I left Hank with Tyler while I headed to Steele Lumber to meet Blake Steele about the job in his offices. I'd worked in marketing in the city, but I was willing to start anywhere. I just wanted money coming in so I could keep building my savings. I'd need to buy my own house eventually. When Kara and Tyler didn't need two extra bodies at their house, taking up space.

Kara had presented me moving in with them as me helping her with the twins and Tyler, but Tyler was doing so much better. And Kara was the strongest person I knew. She never needed anything. I suspected her framing it as me helping them was a ploy, but on the off chance that she did need my help, I was going to be there.

Saving for the future had been an obsession of mine since I was a kid, so free housing or not, I needed a job. It didn't matter if it wasn't in my field. I had my doubts about whether I'd ever find something local in my field. That was okay, though. I could eventually work virtually and make things happen through old connections. Everything would be fine.

Steele Lumber was a huge place on the side of town opposite Isaac's ranch. A big dirt lot acted as parking, and beyond that, there were all kinds of buildings and things that I didn't recognize. There was a constant drone of what I guessed was a saw, or saws, and the scent of wood hung pleasantly in the air. In front of everything stood a small house that had a Steele Lumber sign hanging in front of it.

Assuming that was where I needed to go, I let myself in and found myself in a hectic office. A teenager was in the middle of a pile of papers, her eyes wide as she spotted me. Her blue hair was standing on end and she had trouble getting her hands up to her earbuds to take them out.

"Hey!"

I smiled and waved. "Hey. I'm here for an interview with Blake."

She sank into her pile, relief clear on her face. "Oh, thank god. I thought you were going to need something from me."

I laughed and shook my head. "Are you okay? You need some help getting up? Or...climbing out?"

"Um. Actually. I'm just going to stay down here for now. I don't like that desk. It's got bad vibes from the other lady who works here. She's gone for now, but that desk is haunted, I'm pretty sure."

I nodded. "Got it. Haunted desk."

"Hannah! James Ranier said he's been trying to get through on the office line for two hours. Did you take the phone off the hook again?"

I turned to see who was coming out of the office and froze. Isaac. Frowning, I moved closer to him. "Hey! What are you doing here?"

His brow unfurrowed as he looked me over and a smile stretched his lips. "Working?"

"She's here to interview for Vicki's job. Please hire her and get rid of Vicki for good!"

Isaac sent an exasperated look at the teenager. "Hannah!"

"What? I mean it."

"Come on, let's go to my office." He pointed me into the room he just came from. "Hannah, put the phone back on the hook."

I stopped just inside the door and watched as he pulled it closed and turned to face me. I stepped into his chest, unable to stay away from him. Rubbing his chest, I breathed him in. Something was different. He smelled like cedar and leather. I looked his face over and frowned. "You cut your hair."

His hands rested on my hips, and he shook his head. He opened his mouth to speak when I realized his lips were unscarred. There was also a spot of brown marring his right eye. He wasn't Isaac.

"Oh, god!" I jerked away from him and held out my hands. "I am so sorry. You're not Isaac. I thought you were. I'm so, so sorry."

He laughed easily and rubbed his beard. He really was the spitting image of Isaac and Julian. The third triplet. His hair was shorter than Isaac's, but they really were almost identical. "Hey, you didn't hurt my feelings any. Blake."

I was going to kill Kara. She'd known she was sending me into Isaac's brother and hadn't warned me. I'd just practically rubbed myself all over the man. "Mallory. Again, I am so sorry."

He gestured to the chair across from his and sat down himself. "I take it you know my brother."

I felt my cheeks flame and nodded. "Um, yes. I...I'm sorry. Can we just start over? This might go down in history as the most mortifying job interview ever and I just want to pretend it happened to someone else."

Laughing easily, Blake nodded. "Sure. It's nice to meet you, Mallory. Kara's little sister. She said you worked in marketing."

I nodded jerkily. "I did. For the past ten years."

"You just recently got into town, yeah?"

I nodded. "I did."

He leaned back in his chair and smiled. "Where'd you meet Isaac?"

I wanted the earth to open up and eat me. "Kara threw a party for my son. He turned one, but she threw him a party like he was turning twenty-one. She invited Isaac."

"What's his name?"

The question threw me and I stammered. "H-Hank. Hank Wesley."

"Family name?"

"My grandfather." I straightened in my chair and pushed my hair behind my ears. "Um. I worked in several offices in the last ten years. I know how to run one and I'm good at it."

Blake nodded. "Did Kara tell you it's just until Vicki is off maternity leave? Contrary to what my cousin's daughter wants, Vicki is staying."

"She told me. That's fine. I just want something. The idea of not working stresses me out."

Blake leaned forward and ran his eyes over my face. The motion felt too familiar after I'd pressed against him. It didn't help that he looked identical to a man I'd spent the night with two days before. "Are you dating Isaac?"

I coughed and shook my head. "No. I don't date. I have Hank."

"No dating?"

"No."

Silence stretched between us, and I cleared my throat, wondering what the hell he was thinking. I worried that he could see the truth, that I'd been with both of his brothers. I was terrible.

"Well, I'm available for the job if you need me. I know you're busy, so I won't keep you." I stood up, ending the awkward interview just as awkwardly.

"Mallory—"

I forced a smile and backed towards the door. "Thanks for the interview! Have a great day."

Practically running out of the building, I didn't even bother waving goodbye to Hannah. I just hurried to my car, jumped in, and hurried out of there. I was going to kill Kara. I was also going to die of shame. I wasn't sure which was going to happen first, but I hoped I got to Kara before I keeled over.

Not only had I embarrassed myself, I'd cost myself the job. No way was Blake going to hire me after that display. I was a freak. A bumbling freak. I cringed all the way home, unable to stop thinking about it. That had been awful.

Before I even got all the way home, though, Kara was calling me. I answered with an angry growl. "I'm going to murder you when I see you."

She giggled. "Save your anger. Blake just called me and asked me to have you call him."

I frowned. "Why? That interview was a nightmare."

"I don't know, Mallory. I'm not a mind reader."

"You're dead."

She laughed. "What'd you do?"

"I rubbed all over him before I realized he wasn't Isaac!" I screamed. "Oh, my god, Kara! Saying it out loud just makes it worse. I think I have to leave town. I can't live here."

Snorting and cackling, she laughed hard enough that I heard her wheezing and I knew she was wiping tears. "Oh, god. I had no idea it would be so good."

"I really do hate you. You're a terrible sister."

"Does this mean you are going to date Isaac?"

"What? Where did you get that from?"

"Well, you saw who you thought was him and rubbed against him. That's strange behavior for a woman intent on not dating a man."

I grunted. "Mind your business."

"Call Blake. I'll text you his number." She laughed. "Try not to sext him while you're at it, okay?"

She hung up before I could swear at her. A second later, my phone beeped, and I opened the message as soon as I was in the driveway of the house.

Despite not wanting to call, I did. I did it with my head against the steering wheel, though. Cringing, I waited while it rang with my breath held.

"Mallory?"

I cleared my throat and nodded. Then, realizing he couldn't see me, I groaned. "Yes."

"Can you start tomorrow?" He sounded like he was laughing. "Hannah could really use help, and if I miss another call, I'm going to murder her, and her mother would be pissed. So, please, help me."

I sat up, confused. "What? You want to hire me?"

"I do."

I hesitated. "Are you sure?"

Outright laughing, he was clearly amused by me. "Pretty sure."

"I... Okay." I cleared my throat. "I can start tomorrow."

"Great."

"Um. I just... I'm sorry about how awkward the interview was today. That's not how I typically act."

"No? I thought it was cute." He cleared his throat and grunted. "Not saying that as your boss, of course."

I felt like my face was burning off my skull. "It was just a little weird with what happened and then with, um, Isaac."

"You mean when you felt me up?"

I groaned. "Let's not call it that."

"When you tried to undress me with your eyes, and hands?"

"Definitely not that. Let's just never talk about it again."

He chuckled softly, the sound oddly intimate to my perverted ears. "Or we could talk about it over dinner."

My eyebrows just about shot through the roof of my car. "Sorry, what?"

"Dinner. You and me. This is completely apart from work shit, so if you're not interested, it doesn't affect your job. I'm not a complete asshole."

I held the phone away from my mouth and silently shrieked. What the hell was going on with the men in that family? Pulling the phone back, I composed myself and tried to politely explain that I'd had sex with his brother. Not mentioning the fact that I'd had sex with two of his brothers. "So. You remember the part where I was familiar with your brother? That is still a thing."

"Seeing him?"

"No, that I was familiar with him."

"So, you aren't seeing him?"

I stammered. "I...I don't know."

"I don't mind, either way. Just let me know." He suddenly swore. "Jesus, Hannah is going to ruin me. See you in the morning."

Chapter Nine

I spent the night wondering what the hell Blake meant when he said he didn't mind that I was seeing his brother. He'd still want to take me out to dinner? My brain hurt from running circles. If he really thought I was sleeping with Isaac, why would he want to pursue me? It made no sense. Maybe he was just an asshole who wanted to chase the women his brother chased, but he hadn't seemed like that horrible of a guy. What did I know, though?

I also tossed and turned plenty, wondering what I was doing. I knew I needed to stay away from Julian, but I was involving myself in his life in ways that put me too close to him. I was getting wrapped up with both of his brothers. He'd probably come around at some point and then I was going to be there, waiting with his child. Maybe he wouldn't even remember me. He definitely wouldn't automatically put the numbers together and realize Hank was his kid. The risks were there, though.

I was a nervous wreck by the time I got to Steele Lumber that morning. Hank was with Kara at work for the day, so I didn't have to worry about him being in good hands, but I missed him. I hated being away from him for such a long period of time during the day. I was already planning on sneaking over during my lunch break to see him. I was also overwhelmed by knowing I was walking into an office with Blake.

I'd been too distracted and freaked out the day before to truly appreciate just how handsome he was, but I knew it was there, waiting on me. How three brothers could all be so beautiful was beyond unfair to the rest of the world. They'd stolen the beauty from at least ten other men, I was sure.

Steele Lumber was already loud and active when I got to the parking lot and stiffened my back enough to walk into the office. Hannah was asleep in her pile on the floor, almost as if she'd never left. I walked towards her and cleared my throat. "Hannah?"

She bolted upright and looked around, panic on her face until she saw me. "Oh, thank god. I thought you were going to be Blake."

I saw she was wearing the same clothes as the day before, and it seemed like she really had slept in her pile of paperwork all night. "Um. Do you need some help?"

She climbed to her feet, and I saw that she was taller than me, which was rare. I was five foot nine, without heels, and she had a good six inches on me. Her lanky body unfolded to reveal the waif-like figure of a model. "I can't believe I fell asleep here again. Blake is going to murder me. I have to run home and change. Do you think you can cover for me until I get back?"

I shrugged. "Sure. I'll say you went to get coffee?"

"Not coffee. I hate coffee." She shrugged. "Just tell him I got my period."

I pointed at the pile. "Can I do something with this while you're gone?"

"Um, sure. Whatever. I'll be back!"

I stood there, looking around the office, wondering what I was supposed to do. Blake wasn't there, Hannah had fled, and there didn't seem to be anyone else around. On cue, the phone rang.

"Steele Lumber." I shrugged to myself, just guessing at how Blake liked the phone to be answered.

"Hey, Mallory. I had to run an errand this morning. I'll be in after lunch. I would say that Hannah could show you around, but that seems like a bad plan."

I smiled and stared down at the pile of paperwork again. "What's with the pile?"

He snorted. "Pretty sure it's her safety blanket. I asked her to scan and shred all that three weeks ago."

"Got it. I can do that. Where do I scan it to?" I knelt in front of the pile and started sorting the papers closest to me. I listened while he gave me information to log onto the computer in his office and directed me on where to save which files. "Anything else I can do?"

"There's paperwork for you to fill out on my desk for the hire. Just fill it out and leave it there. I'll handle it when I get in." He paused for a second. "I'll see you soon, Mallory."

I hung up and ignored the shiver that ran down my spine. Getting to work right away was easy. The work was tedious but simple. I scanned papers for hours after filling out my paperwork while sitting at Blake's desk. I sat in his big desk chair while I organized the scans on his computer and let the leather mold to my body when I did take short breaks. I lost track of time and was humming to myself, bent over the dwindling pile of papers, when a throat cleared from behind me.

Screaming, I jumped and spun around, my hands coming up in a defensive stance. My heart racing, I found Blake grinning. "You almost gave me a heart attack!"

He leaned against Vicki's desk and kept right on grinning. "I didn't try to sneak in. You just didn't hear me over your singing."

"I wasn't singing."

"Sounded like singing to me." He bit his lip and his eyes crinkled as he fought a laugh. "Well. Something like singing."

I scoffed. "That's not very nice."

"I'll just say it's a really good thing you're so beautiful." He straightened and looked at the pile that I'd nearly taken out completely. "Holy shit. You did all of that already?"

Blushing from his compliment, I nodded. "Yes, sir."

His eyes darkened for a moment as they met mine, but the heat I thought I saw was gone before I could fully examine it. "Just Blake here."

I raised my eyebrows but just nodded. "I filled out the paperwork on your desk, too. And I'm supposed to tell you that Hannah got her period and is coming in soon."

"She was asleep in here again, wasn't she?"

"No?"

He shrugged. "It's fine. I'm not mad at her for sleeping in the office. I'm mad that she won't leave her asshole boyfriend who kicks her out of their apartment all the time."

"She's old enough to live with her boyfriend? I thought she was a kid."

"She's eighteen." He rubbed his hand down his face. "Still a kid if you ask me, but her mom doesn't think so."

I frowned and scooped up the last of the papers on the floor. "He just kicks her out?"

Blake sighed heavily and shrugged. "I guess so. She won't really talk to me about it much. She's afraid I'll kill her boyfriend. It's a valid fear."

I followed him as he walked into his office, lost in the conversation. "Speaking as someone who went through a long line of asshole boyfriends, she won't leave him until she's good and done with him. Even if that means she gets her feelings annihilated in the process."

He'd paused in the middle of his office and I bumped straight into his back. "You cleaned."

I straightened myself and cringed. I was an idiot. "No, I just dusted a bit."

He turned to face me and tilted his head. "You don't have to clean. Or cover for Hannah. Or date me if you don't want to. I don't want you doing anything that makes you uncomfortable or seems out of the job description."

"I know." I bit my upper lip, an unattractive tick I had when feeling nervous. "I just had the time and was waiting around on your computer to boot up, so I dusted. It's nothing."

He looked my face over like he was trying to make sense of something. "Vicki's going to come in this afternoon for a few minutes and walk you through the job. I don't think you'll have any trouble with anything."

I nodded and backed away. "Great! I'm just going to finish these scans, I guess."

"You can keep using my desk. I'm going out to the shop to check on things. I'll be back in a while." Walking towards me, he gently put his hand on my arm and then scooted around me. "No more cleaning, Mallory."

I let out a big breath as soon as he left and sank into one of his office chairs. Being around him wasn't easy. He looked so much like Isaac and Julian, but there was something so uniquely him that it threw me off. My body didn't know what to feel and my brain didn't know what to think. There was a tension between us that I didn't understand. How could I have that same tension with two different men at the same time?

I rolled my eyes at myself. Of course, it was possible. People slept with more than one person at the same time. Or, not at the same time, I thought with a blush. Stupid. I was no virgin, but there I was, feeling giggly and red-faced over a set of brothers that I had no business being near.

Shaking off the distraction, I focused on working. I'd just finished organizing the last file on Blake's desk when he strolled back in and joined me.

"Carry on. I just have to grab something."

I stood up as he was speaking and ended up blocking us both in behind his desk. "Oh, sorry. I'd just finished. I'll just scoot past."

He leaned into the closet behind his desk and grabbed a shirt. I tried to squeeze past him, but my ass definitely rubbed across his hip as I moved by. His answering swear and sharp intake of breath sent me scrambling to the other side of the office.

"Sorry! Jesus, I'm a mess. I didn't mean to do that, I promise." I groaned and shook my head. "I'm pretty sure you could sue me for sexual harassment at this point."

He moved towards me, his big body graceful. He almost looked like a lion stalking its prey. "I'm going to say this one time and one time only."

I held my breath as he stopped right in front of me and rested his hands on my shoulders.

"You don't ever need to apologize for rubbing your body against me. It's never going to be unwelcomed." He stroked his hand up and cupped my neck. "And if anyone is getting sued here, it's me, because I shouldn't be touching you."

My stomach fluttered and my heart sped up. I licked my lips and shook my head, trying to make myself think. "I'm not going to sue you."

Stepping closer, Blake ran his thumb over the base of my throat. "I need to get out of here."

I looked up at him and nodded. "I should get to work, too."

Even closer, he settled his other hand on my hip and leaned into me. "I lied earlier."

I swayed into him and braced myself with my hands on his chest. "When?"

"I liked your singing."

"Blake! I'm here! Did Mallory tell you I had my period?" Hannah's voice called through the office loudly. "Hey! Where's my pile?"

Sighing, Blake stepped away from me and smiled. "Sounds like you might be in trouble."

I blew out a shaky breath and nodded. "I'd fucking say."

CHAPTER TEN

I made it through the rest of the day without running into Blake's chest again. Vicki showed up and walked me through all of her duties while eyeing me up and down. Hannah was right about her. Vicki wasn't a very nice woman. She kept me away from my boss, though, so I appreciated her, even in her moodiness.

Back at home, I took Hank from Kara and held him while I rested on the couch. He was content to just play with my hair while I held him, and it was the most peace I'd felt all day. I was still enjoying him when a knock sounded on the door. Kara called out to me a second later, and I felt a flutter in my stomach, wondering who was there for me. Isaac, or Blake. Dismay hit me as I realized I didn't know which one I'd rather it be.

I adjusted Hank and went to see who was there. Finding Isaac, I smiled. I also realized, though, that I would've been happy to see Blake, too. What was wrong with me?

"Hey." Isaac's slow smile sent warmth pooling between my thighs. He laughed as Hank reached for him and happily took my son from me. "Have you eaten?"

I was about to answer when Kara appeared from behind me. "She hasn't eaten. She's famished, just starving. You have to take her and feed her right now!"

I grunted as she pushed me out of the house. "Kara!"

"And just hand that baby back to me. I had to share him with my coworkers today so I didn't get as much time as I needed. You kids go eat and I'll see you later, Mal."

I took Hank before she could and held him to my chest. "I've barely seen him at all today."

Isaac shrugged. "Bring him with us."

I thought about what we might end up doing when I went with him and nearly choked. "On second thought, he should spend some time bonding with his Aunt Kara."

Kara laughed and took him from me. "That's what I thought. You kids have fun now."

Before I could even grab my purse, she shut the door in my face. I sighed and looked back at Isaac. "This is your fault."

The door opened a crack and my purse and shoes were shoved out at me. Kara laughed maniacally. "We won't wait up on you!"

Isaac helped me step into my shoes and then led me to his truck, laughing at how I'd just gotten kicked out of my house. "Dating you will be easy as long as you live with Kara."

I scowled at him even as my body readied itself for him. One night of sex with him and I was already eager to get back to it, despite what I'd been telling myself about not doing it again. "I don't date."

He opened the door for me and then lifted me into the truck, stepping between my thighs before I could get settled the correct way in the seat. His hands stroked my legs, and he easily took my mouth in a fierce kiss.

I arched my hips into him and opened my mouth for him, eager for more. Grabbing his hair, I pressed my chest into his and moaned his name. I felt like I'd been turned on for days on end and a release was in sight. I needed it. I needed him.

Isaac rubbed his knuckle over my core, through my leggings, and then pulled back with a growl. "Unless you want to be bent over right in the driveway, I suggest we stop now."

I licked my lips, tasting his kiss, and nodded. "Yep, you're right. Just don't touch me again right now."

He nodded and backed away. "Got it."

He got in and drove away from Kara's house, his knuckles white on the steering wheel. I leaned against the door, trying to keep as much space between us as possible. I didn't even notice he wasn't driving to his house until he parked in front of the diner on Main Street.

"What are we doing here?"

He opened his door and got out, putting even more space between us. "Having a real date."

I groaned. "Isaac."

Laughing, he closed his door and walked around to mine. "That almost sounded like a whine, Mal."

I wasn't going to give him the pleasure of me begging to be taken to his house and pleasured. Plus, I was a proper lady. Or at least I pretended to be at times. I could have dinner with him without humping his leg at the table. I had resolve and self-control. "Lead the way."

He took my hand and pulled me after him into the diner. The place was packed for the dinner crowd, but Isaac managed to find a booth in the back for us. He sat down in the booth next to me and pressed into me. "So. This is dating."

I laughed, despite myself. "I don't like you very much."

"I'll grow on you."

"Like a mold?"

He wrapped his arm around me and played with my hair. "If I have to. We really could've brought Hank, you know?"

I cut my eyes at him. "I thought we were going to your house to make burgers, if you know what I mean. I didn't think he needed that trauma."

"Make burgers?"

I elbowed him and ignored the blush forming on my face. "You suck and you're having too much fun with this."

A shadow fell over the table and I looked up to see Blake standing with a milkshake in his hand. He grinned, even as the blush on my face grew darker. My heart nearly quit working at the embarrassment of being in the same place as both of them.

"I saw you two come in and thought I might crash your date."

Isaac nodded to the seat opposite us and grinned. "We were just talking about what we were going to order. I want a burger."

I placed both hands on the tabletop and thought about what the consequences would be if I just ducked under the table and ran out of there. Seeing them so close together let me see more of their differences, but it was still almost uncanny how similar they were. My brain was struggling.

"Did Mallory tell you about work? She's kind of amazing." Blake smiled at me and took a sip of his shake before going on. "I know you're severely underutilized in that role, but I'll keep an eye out and see if anyone might need marketing work."

"Same." Isaac shrugged. "If I decide to open up the ranch for a weekend experience thing, I'll hire you to do the marketing for it."

I nodded and looked between the two of them. What was happening? I shifted in my seat and was saved from blurting out my thoughts by the waitress showing up.

"Blake, Isaac." She looked at me, her kind eyes narrowing slightly as she tried to place me. "I don't think I've met you before."

"Mallory Russell. I'm new in town." I sent her a kind smile, despite the turmoil banging around in my head.

"She's Kara's little sister." Isaac tugged a lock of my hair and then stroked the side of my neck ever so gently, giving me goosebumps all over.

"And Kara let her little sister out with the two of you?" Grinning, the woman looked at me and held out her hand. "Nice to meet you, Mallory. I'm Berna. Berna Jones. I run this place and have for about a hundred years. If these two give you any trouble, let me know."

"You know we're never any trouble, Berna." Blake took another drink of his shake and winked at me. "Never the bad kind, anyway."

"Lord. What do you three want? I can't stay around this much testosterone for too long, or my body will think it's interested in that again."

I laughed and found myself grateful for Berna being there to break some of the tension I was feeling. We ordered, and then I couldn't kick the giggles after Berna left. Everything just felt so outrageous.

"What's so funny?"

I eyed Blake and then Isaac. "This. I feel like I'm on a date with the two of you."

Isaac leaned into me and brushed his lips over my ear. "Berna seemed to think this much testosterone was tempting."

I met Blake's eyes and felt heat ripple through my body. I looked back at Isaac and sighed into him as he kissed me gently. Then, the drinks were being dropped off and Berna was making told-you-so noises. I sat back in my seat and tucked my hair behind my ears. What the fuck was happening?

I was a wreck. I was turned on; my body felt like it was running about a thousand degrees higher than it should've been. My heart was racing, and I had the curious feeling that something big was coming. I felt drunk, tipsy on the men at my table.

Berna was right about there being too much testosterone. It made it hard for a woman to process her thoughts very well. All I knew was that I'd been in Briar's Point for less than a week and I already had a man kissing me like he'd been doing it for years. All while another watched and made eyes at me like he was in line for next.

"Um..." I looked between the two of them and raised my eyebrows. "What the fuck is going on?"

Blake chuckled and looked to his brother. "Isaac?"

Isaac took a long drink of his tea and then met my gaze. "Nothing that you don't want. Except for the dates. I did kind of push that on you."

"Nothing I don't want? What do you mean?"

"We should probably have this conversation elsewhere." Blake nodded to the table of people right behind us, and I noticed that the woman at the booth behind us was practically breaking her neck to get closer to us.

Isaac nodded. "We'll talk tonight. For now, let's enjoy our date. Let us get to know you better."

I motioned between the three of us. "*Our* date?"

Blake stroked his beard and seemed to be lost in thought for a few seconds before meeting Isaac's gaze. They seemed to communicate without words, and then Blake nodded and looked at me. "Only if you want it."

A wash of shock rolled over me, but I was ashamed to admit that under the shock was a tidal wave of desire. I didn't know what was going on with me, but what they seemed to be suggesting, what Blake had hinted at before on the phone, was that they would share. I didn't know whether to be more flattered than I'd ever been in my life, or if I should let them know that I wasn't a family-sized bucket of fried chicken to be passed back and forth.

I realized I'd been holding my breath and sucked in a huge gulp of air. I looked around the diner and then back at the oversized mountain men sitting with me. They were a walking, talking wet dream, and I was pretty sure my mind had conjured them, but I was a normal woman. A mom. I wasn't someone who dated two men at the same time. I'd been a little wild before I'd had Hank but having sex with two brothers was not something I'd ever considered. Three brothers, if I counted the past.

I shifted again and squeezed my thighs together, searching for even the slightest bit of relief for my aching core. My body knew what it wanted. It liked the sound of both men pleasing me. It had no qualms.

Isaac rested his hand on my thigh under the table and leaned into me again. "Why don't we go to my house and just talk? Would that help any?"

His warmth and the gentle way he handled me were exactly what I needed at that moment. When I nodded, he looked to

Blake, and then Blake left the table, leaving us alone. Instantly, I worried I'd somehow given him the impression that I wanted Blake gone. I opened my mouth to protest, but Isaac's smile cut me off.

"He's just telling Berna we want our orders to go. Come on. We'll meet him at the ranch."

Chapter Eleven

In the truck on the way to Isaac's, I peppered him with questions I'd been too nervous to ask in front of both him and Blake together. "So, you want to share me?"

Isaac grunted. "I don't know if share is the right word."

"So, he'll take me on Mondays, Wednesdays, and Fridays and you get the rest of the week?"

"Not exactly."

"Is there a schedule?"

"No, Mallory. There's no schedule."

"Is this dating? This feels a lot like dating."

"This is dating."

"I don't date."

He sighed. "We're dating."

"You can't just decide that."

"Hey, Mallory?" He waited until I answered him. "Do you want to come over to my house tonight and hang out? We could watch a movie or play a board game."

I narrowed my eyes. "Okay?"

"That's dating. We're dating."

"And I'm dating Blake, too?"

"If you want to be. And I get the feeling you want to be."

I winced. "What is wrong with me?"

"Nothing. You're fucking perfect."

"I think I might be a sexual deviant." I groaned. "I can't sleep with all three of a set of triplets. That's got to be some kind of thing. Like an illegal thing. What is wrong with me, Isaac? Am I a slut? I am. I'm a slut."

"You're not a slut. Jesus, woman, just take it easy for a second." Isaac turned onto the road leading to the ranch and shook his head. "You're not a slut. Do you understand me?"

I sighed. "You're awfully bossy for a man I barely know."

"We'll change part of that."

"I'm assuming not the bossy part."

He parked in front of the house and came around to open my door for me. Instead of helping me out, he captured my mouth in a kiss that sent desire coursing through my body. "If you ever feel uncomfortable at all, tell me. Tell us."

I pulled his hair out of the low bun he had it tied back in and stroked it. It was silky under my fingers. "Is tonight your night?"

He picked me up and wrapped my legs around his waist to carry me inside. "Our night."

I wiggled against him. "I'm too heavy for you to carry, Isaac. Put me down."

"You're not too heavy. You're just right."

"I'm—" I stopped and looked down at him. "Our night?"

"If you want it."

I went quiet as he carried me into the living room and sank onto the couch with me straddling him. Even the distraction of our bodies rubbing together didn't work on me. "So... Really sharing?"

He laughed and then cocked his head to the side. "Sounds like Blake's here."

"You mean... All three of us together? Not like separate nights." I was starting to panic slightly. "Do the two of you...?"

"God, no." He shivered under me and shook his head. "No, never. That's not okay."

I sighed. "Okay. So, just me, then?"

He gripped my hips and pulled me tighter against his growing erection. "Just you."

"This is insane."

The door opened and closed and then Blake sauntered into the room. He looked at me sitting on his brother's lap and leaned against the doorway. "What's insane?"

I blushed and tried to shift off of Isaac, but Blake shook his head.

"Stay. You're making my brother very happy right now." He pushed off the wall and sat next to us on the couch. His thigh rubbed against my leg and his eyes roamed my body freely. "So, what's insane?"

I scoffed. "This. You two wanting to...share...me." Even saying the words was hard to do in front of them. "How does that even work?"

Isaac grinned. "You want details?"

"No." I hesitated. "Yes. Before I decide anything, I need to know everything."

Blake rested his hand on my thigh and stretched his legs out in front of him. "What kind of details do you want?"

Feeling three different hands on my body, I couldn't deny the pooling of wetness at my core. I was beyond turned on by the two of them touching me. "Do you two do this often?"

Isaac grunted. "Not anymore."

"We did it more when we were younger. We had a couple of girlfriends together."

"Girlfriends?"

Isaac laughed and looked at his brother. "She's against dating."

"I think you might be dating." Blake reached out and stroked his hand over my cheek. "The most important thing in all of this is that it's whatever you want. You make the rules. Except maybe about the dating."

I found myself leaning into his hand, searching for more of his touch. "And the sex?"

Isaac leaned forward and pressed his lips to my neck. "The sex."

Blake's thumb trailed over my lip. "What Isaac is trying to say is that the sex is whatever you want from us. We're here to please you. If you want us one at a time, or if you want us both at the same time, it's up to you."

Isaac kissed along my jawline. "Or you can let us take control."

I shivered. I'd always liked a more dominant partner in sex. Could I do it? Could I have sex with both of them? What did that mean? What did it mean for me in everyday life? "What about work?"

"You're thinking about work right now?" Blake laughed. "It doesn't change anything. I don't touch you at work if you don't want me to."

I swallowed around a lump of nerves. "And if I want you to?"

"Then it's a good day." He sat up and leaned closer to me. "Do you want us, Mallory?"

I looked at both of them, so dangerously sexy and attentive. I knew I did. I wanted to explore the desires I was feeling. I knew it wasn't the best idea to explore those desires with men who were technically Hank's uncles, but I wanted them both. I'd never wanted two men at the same time; I'd never even delved into the possibility through porn. Yet, I couldn't deny the need I felt.

"It doesn't mean we're dating." I nervously gathered my hair and twisted it in my hand. "I'm nervous, I guess. But I think I want this. Is that crazy? I mean, what does that say about me?"

"It says that you're a sexual being with desires and urges that are going to be met by two men." Isaac took my hair from me and ran it through his fingers. "You're so beautiful. This hair, though. This hair makes me crazy."

Blake grunted in agreement. "Come here, Mallory."

I practically shook with the sexual tension flowing through my body, but I reached over and braced my hands on his shoulders as Isaac eased me into his brother's lap. Straddling Blake, I licked my lips and looked back at Isaac to make sure it was okay.

Blake lightly grabbed my chin and pulled my face to his. "We're both here with you. And we're both going to love your body tonight. Right now, I want to taste you, though, Mal."

He pressed his lips against mine, and I sighed into his kiss. I was kissing him in front of Isaac, and knowing that Isaac was watching sent tingles racing all over my body. I shifted against Blake and tried to kiss him deeper, but he pulled back and kissed down my throat instead. I shuddered as his teeth raked over my tender skin and arched my hips into his without a second thought.

Isaac caught the hem of my shirt and pulled it up and off. His low growl of approval was paired with his mouth on my shoulder. "Fucking beautiful."

Blake kissed me again and gripped the back of my head to deepen it. He stroked his tongue into my mouth, and I felt his erection press into my core as it grew. He groaned and pulled back to look into my eyes. "What do you want us to do, baby?"

I felt myself preen at the soft name. I felt sexy and cared for at that moment, more than I ever had been before. "I want you to be in control."

"Stand up for me. I want to see you."

Isaac helped me stand up and stood behind me. He caressed his hands over my stomach and up to my breasts. "She's stunning."

I moaned when he found my nipples and plucked at them through my lace bra. When that wasn't enough for him, he unhooked the bra and pushed it down my shoulders, revealing my naked upper half to Blake.

"Fuck." Blake sat forward and rested his elbows on his knees. "More."

Kissing my neck and shoulders, Isaac stroked my nipples and lightly pinched them, showing Blake how it made me squirm and squeeze my thighs together. Reaching down to my leggings, he tucked his hands into the sides and pushed them down my thighs. My panties went with them and after stepping out of them, I was completely naked in front of the two of them.

My heart raced as I was exposed. I was so wet that I felt like they could probably see it leaking out of me.

Blake reached for me, but instead of pulling me back on him like I had been, he turned me around and pulled me down on him, facing Isaac. He hooked my legs on either side of his and Isaac growled as he got a full view of my core, stretched open and exposed.

With my back pressed against his chest, I looked back at Blake and moaned when he took my chin and tilted my mouth up to his. His kiss was demanding and strong. His grip on my chin moved down to my throat as he held me where he wanted me. He took his time and stroked my tongue with his, sending me spiraling.

Squeezing my thighs to ease the tension wasn't an option with my thighs stretched open, so I was left to shake and twist on his lap as neediness took over my brain. Suddenly it didn't matter that there were two of them and that was scandalous. It just mattered that they were going to touch me and ease the ache I was feeling in my core.

Chapter Twelve

Isaac's hands massaged my calves and then stroked up my thighs. His breath caressed the spots his hands abandoned and then centered over my core. "You're so wet, Mal. Is this all for us?"

Blake stroked down my stomach and tightly cupped my sex while still holding my face towards him. "Tell Isaac what you want from him."

With a shiver taking over my body, I arched my back to present myself to Isaac, but Blake's hand didn't allow much movement. When he didn't let up, I moaned and realized I was going to have to say the words. I was already panting from need, so my voice was husky when I spoke. "I want you to lick me."

Blake slipped his fingers into my folds and circled my clit. "You're dripping, baby. I'm jealous of Isaac getting all of this to himself."

Isaac growled and pushed two thick fingers into my core. "Fuck, I missed your body. How is that even possible after just a few days?"

I moaned loudly and reached for him, but Blake lifted his arm to wrap around my waist, trapping my arms and holding me in place. The sensation added to everything I was feeling and heightened my pleasure. I felt like I was already on the edge of a massive orgasm. "Please."

Tipping my mouth back up to his, Blake captured my mouth in a heated kiss that stole my breath. He sucked my bottom lip into his mouth and nipped it before stroking it with his tongue and kissing me deep again. His beard rubbed my chin and the skin around my mouth, but I found myself wanting even more.

Isaac covered my clit with his mouth and sucked, ripping a cry from my throat even as Blake kissed it away. His fingers pumped into me and then pulled out so his tongue could do the same. Then, he pushed his fingers in again and did that until I wanted to scream. Just when I thought he'd pushed me into insanity, he covered my clit and flicked his tongue over it hard and fast while his fingers filled me. As he rocketed me towards an orgasm, I felt another of his fingers stroke over my back entrance, wet with my juices. I jerked against the intrusion, but it instantly sent my body soaring into an almost painful orgasm.

Blake kissed down to my ear, his arms still holding me in place as I shook. "That's it, baby. Come for us."

Isaac licked me through my orgasm and only stopped when my shaking body settled slightly. Then, he pulled his fingers out of me and stretched up to kiss me, letting me taste myself on his tongue. "You're so sweet. I could eat you all day long."

Blake let my arms go and I wasted no time in reaching up and undoing Isaac's pants. Our night together had shown me that I really loved the way he moaned when I took him into my mouth and I wanted to hear him go weak for me. I slipped to my knees on the hard floor and pulled his pants down enough to pull his cock free. Still so wildly turned on, I leaned into him and took as much of his length as I could into my mouth.

Isaac swore and tangled his hands in my hair, using his grip to pump my mouth up and down his length once before pulling me off of him and turning me towards Blake. "Show him how good you are."

I settled between Blake's thighs and watched him as he unbuttoned his pants and pulled his zipper down. My body pulsed, and I moaned when Isaac reached under me to bring me up on all fours. His fingers teased my opening as Blake freed his cock and moved forward on the couch so I could reach it. I licked his head and sucked it into my mouth before letting it pop out. Licking the underside of his shaft from base to tip, I then took him into my mouth and lowered my head until the tip of him brushed the back of my throat. It was a skill I'd perfected with a boyfriend when I was younger that I'd always been proud of.

Blake swore and grabbed my hair into his big fists. "Jesus, Mallory. Isaac said you had a golden mouth, but that's a fucking understatement."

I sucked my way back up and then bobbed my head up and down his head for a minute, teasing his slit with my tongue. I was taking him deep into my mouth again when I felt Isaac running his cock through my folds. I moaned, and Blake swore even louder.

Isaac pushed the tip of his cock into me and gripped my ass. He slid in slowly, his girth feeling thicker from the new angle. He squeezed my cheeks, spreading my ass and then pushing it back together. When he finally bottomed out in me, I was moaning so much on Blake's shaft that he finally pulled my mouth off of him with a curse and tipped my chin up so he could see me and I could see him.

"You're too fucking good at that."

I rested my cheek on his thigh as Isaac pulled out and then thrust back in. Slow and hard, he fucked me while I clung to his brother's thighs. When Blake offered me his cock again, I worked him into my mouth and stroked him with my tongue. He used my hair to work my head up and down on his shaft, taking my mouth in rhythm with his brother.

Isaac spread my knees open wider and reached around my waist to find my clit as he thrust into me. He thrust harder, sending my head forward on Blake's cock. My body squeezed around him, my pleasure already shooting through the roof. "That's it, Mal. Come for me again. Come on my cock."

Hearing the dirty words and being filled at both ends by them was more than I could handle. As his fingers rubbed over my clit, I came apart, screaming around Blake's dick.

Blake pulled himself from my mouth and stood up, pulling me up with him. Isaac settled on the end of the couch as Blake bent me over the arm of it. Thrusting into my core with one strong stroke, he moaned and gripped my hips. "Suck him, baby. Take him into your mouth and finish him while I fill you with my come."

Isaac stroked my hair and face and then pulled my mouth down onto his cock. Still shaking from my orgasm, I did as good as I could. My body felt like one giant nerve ending as I took both of them into my body again. I was almost bent in half to get him into my mouth, but Blake held me steady as he thrust into me.

Hard and fast, he filled me again and again. He was similar to Isaac in size, but he pounded into me like a wild man. The sound of our flesh slapping together filled the room and I moaned at the wildness of it all.

My eyes flew open when I felt Blake's finger circle that same place that Isaac had earlier. With my mouth full of Isaac, I found myself moaning, unsure if I was wanting him to stop or go farther. His finger wet with my fluids, he pressed harder until he slipped inside. His other hand found my clit and caught it between two fingers while he slowly pushed his finger in deeper.

I wiggled and moaned, unsure of the feeling. Isaac responded to all of my moaning by gripping my head and thrusting his hips up to meet my mouth. He filled my mouth and brushed the back of my throat, all while grabbing my breasts and pinching my nipples. My body went higher and higher at the feelings until I thought I'd die if I didn't come again.

Blake pulled his finger out and then thrust it back in, fucking me in both holes. The room was filled with the sounds of our pleasure and it just grew louder as Isaac lifted my head from his cock.

"Are you going to come again for us, Mal?" He kissed me hard and listened to the sounds of my broken cries of pleasure before gripping the base of his cock and letting me take him back into my mouth. As I sucked hard, he swore. "I'm going to come, Mal."

I shook his hands away as he tried to lift my head. I wanted him to come in my mouth. I wanted to please him in every way. My body shook and tightened like a coil as I drew closer to my own orgasm. Blake was setting a punishing rhythm that was taking my breath away.

He pushed another finger into my bottom that sent me flying over the edge. I screamed around Isaac's cock, even as he came hard, filling my mouth. Blake's thrusts missed a beat when my core squeezed around him tightly. He rubbed my clit as I crumbled and then he came with a mighty growl himself.

I swallowed Isaac's seed until I couldn't focus my body. I ended up with my head buried in his lap, the last bit of his come in my hair. I cried out their names as my orgasm rocked me and Blake filled my core with his come. Feeling both of the men coming for me was a power trip, and I couldn't help smiling when I regained function of my muscles.

My core pulsed and milked Blake, pleasure filling me and spilling over. I'd never had an orgasm hit me so hard. I wasn't sure where my body started and ended for a minute as I rode it out.

"Fucking hell." Blake gently pulled his fingers out of me and then slipped his cock free before picking me up and settling us on the couch with Isaac. They held me there, stroking my hair and kissing my shoulders for some time.

When I finally started to come back down to earth, I realized how pleasantly sore my core and bottom were and wondered if I'd walk funny the next day. I sighed happily and enjoyed being held.

"I think you have to marry us now."

Isaac snorted as I lifted my head and rolled my eyes. "Your brother said almost the same thing."

Blake stroked my cheek and smiled. "Doesn't that just show you it's meant to be? After this, you might be stuck with us."

I smiled to myself, blocking out the reality knocking at the back of my brain. "Is it always that good?"

"No. Never." He pulled a blanket off the back of the couch and covered me with it. "You're magic."

I curled more into them and buried my face in Isaac's chest. "I have to go home soon to be with Hank."

"I'll take you on my way home." Blake reached over and held up a piece of my hair that had a suspicious residue in it. "Maybe a shower first, though?"

I cut my eyes at Isaac. "You decorated me."

He easily picked me up and tossed my naked body over his shoulder. Slapping my ass, he carried me towards his bathroom with a call to his brother on the way. "Coming?"

Feeling like truly living up the role I'd landed in, I reached around and stroked him. "I hope so."

Blake stripped as he came into the bathroom. "I think we can help with that."

CHAPTER THIRTEEN

Hannah sat on the floor next to my desk with her feet propped up on the side of my chair. "I just don't understand the point of me answering the phone for him. The only people who call are calling for him. He could just answer and cut out the middleman. It's all about efficiency now."

I finished putting in the timesheet information and then turned to her. "You know, if he did decide to start answering his own calls, you'd be out of a job."

She frowned and sank onto the floor the rest of the way. "Oh."

I laughed and patted her ankle. "You'll get used to the phones someday."

"Nope. People should just text."

Blake strolled into the office and grinned when he saw me. He glanced around, didn't see Hannah, and started to come around towards me. "You look like you had—"

Hannah grunted from having Blake half-step on her. He stumbled and caught himself on the edge of my desk, a frown on his face as he looked down at her. I barely stifled a laugh.

"Hannah, what the hell are you doing down there?"

"Resting! What the hell are you doing stomping around here? You never come over here."

I raised my eyebrows at him. I didn't know what he'd been about to say, but I had a feeling it wasn't going to be work appropriate. I was glad he wasn't acting cold after the night we'd shared, though.

Clearing his throat, Blake backed away. "I was just checking things out. Get off the floor, Hannah. And Mallory, can I see you in my office?"

Hannah mumbled under her breath about not getting up but got up anyway. She sank into the empty chair next to the empty desk she didn't want and sighed. "You're my least favorite triplet right now."

I laughed and stood up. My body ached as I did, muscles I'd never used sore from the new activities. Pushing Blake towards his office so he didn't argue with Hannah, I gasped when he shut the door just to push me against it and kiss me.

It was inappropriate, and I had no intention of letting it happen, but my hands were in his hair and I was kissing him back with everything I had. His hands were on my ass, pulling my hips into his, and I was rubbing myself against his erection. It happened so fast, but not fast enough. I was tempted to pull my dress up and bend over his desk for him.

When he finally pulled away from me, it was just to run his hand up my thigh and under my dress. "You're addictive."

I bit my lip and looked at him through heavy eyes as he slipped his fingers into my panties and found my clit. "We shouldn't be doing this at work."

"We could go back to my place."

I moaned as he worked his fingers expertly over me. "Blake..."

He pressed his mouth into my ear and growled. "I love hearing you cry out my name."

The phone rang somewhere else in the office and I remembered myself. Pushing his hand away, I straightened my dress. Even as my body craved him, I put some distance between us and held up my hands to stop him from closing the gap again. "Not at work. I'm a professional. At least I was."

He groaned and nodded. "Fine. But you should get out of here before I do my best to have you professionally bent over my desk."

I hurried out of his office and into the bathroom to make sure I didn't look like I'd just been caught hooking up. After seeing that I was okay, I went back to my desk and tried to work when all I wanted to do was chase my orgasm with Blake. Or Isaac. I found myself daydreaming about them instead of doing my work.

I was still ignoring the base conversations I needed to have with myself. I was barking up the wrong tree with the Steele brothers, but there was chemistry with them like I'd never felt. They also tapped into all of my base desires, even ones I hadn't known about.

"Do you hear that?"

I looked over at Hannah and shook my head. "No. What?"

She stood up and walked over to the window that overlooked the parking lot. "It's a motorcycle. That means Julian is coming. Man, he's cool."

My back about snapped in half, it went so rigid. "What?"

"There he is!"

I stood up and spun in a little circle, wondering how fast I could get out of the office without him seeing me. "I've got to go."

"You can't leave now. You have to see him. He's got all these tattoos and he's just so cool. None of the other cousins are like him."

I thought about going to the bathroom and hiding, but then I worried about how long he might stay. I could always sneak out the back, but that meant I'd have to sneak past all the windows, including the ones in Blake's office. Then, I'd also have to explain running away.

Before I could decide what I was doing, the door opened and the sounds of heavy boots coming near rattled through the office. I sank to my knees on the ground behind my desk and bent over, trying to hide. It was a stupid idea, but I was desperate.

"Hey, Julian! How are you?" Hannah sounded even younger than she was in her adoration of him.

Julian was quiet, but I could practically feel him standing on the other side of the desk, just existing. "Hey, Han."

I cringed and tried to make myself even smaller. I was an idiot. The exact reason I should've stayed away from the Steele brothers was just on the other side of my desk. I silently banged my head into the floor and thought about how I was going to get out of there. I had to. I couldn't run into Julian.

"Finding anything good down there?"

I jerked when Julian's gruff voice came from over me. Hitting the back of my head on my desk, I winced even as I pretended to find something on the floor under my desk. "Ah, here it is."

"How long are you in town for, Julian?"

Forced out of my hiding spot, I slowly pulled myself to my feet and turned to face him. I didn't have a choice. What else could I do? I sucked in a sharp breath as I did, unprepared for the darkness in his eyes. He was so identical to his brothers, but seeing him again really allowed me to see how different he was. There was just a force of danger around him. His entire body radiated a negative energy that probably acted as a forcefield for most people.

I took in his worn black t-shirt and black jeans and the leather riding gloves he was pulling off. His hair was pushed back with a black bandana and his beard was longer and wilder than his brothers'. He looked like a biker, ready to charge into a bar fight.

"Cammie?"

I took a step backward and cursed my white skin that loved to glow red. It sucked.

Hannah laughed. "Wrong ex lady friend, Julian. This is Mallory. She just started working here."

His eyes narrowed as he took me in. "Mallory?"

I shifted and crossed my arms over my chest. I felt like he would be able to see all of my secrets if I wasn't careful. "That's my name."

"So you're a liar." He shook his head. "What are you doing here?"

Anger surged. "You're kidding, right?"

"No, Cammie, I'm not kidding."

I came up to my full height, in heels, and scowled back at him. Who the hell did he think he was? "My name is Mallory and you can use it, or better yet, don't use it."

"Again, what are you doing here?"

Blake came from his office and spotted the tension between the two of us. "Julian, what's up?"

"Why is she working here?"

Blake frowned and then turned to Hannah. "Hannah, do me a favor and go look for my phone in my truck. I lost it and I'm expecting a call."

Hannah groaned. "Blake! I can see your phone in your pocket."

"Hannah, go."

She stomped out of the office and slammed the door behind her.

Blake then turned to his brother and frowned. "What the fuck is wrong with you? Why are you being an asshole?"

Julian crossed his arms over his chest and shook his head. "Just wondering why the fuck you're hiring my old conquests."

I felt my body heat up and growled. "Do you always think everything is about you? My working here has *nothing* to do with you."

Blake looked me over. "You okay?"

I calmed down slightly when I met his eyes. "Yeah. Fine."

Julian laughed, but there was no humor in it. "Oh, I see."

"What, Julian? What do you see?"

"You're fucking her." Julian sent me a disgusted look. "You making your way through all the Steele men?"

Blake grabbed the front of his brother's shirt and shook him. "That's enough. What's your fucking problem?"

Still scowling at me, he spoke to his brother. "Did you know she was with me before?"

I raised my eyebrows. "I'd hardly say I was with you. A fifteen-minute tryst in your truck barely counts as anything."

Blake bit back a smile and held up his hands. "Okay, this has been fun, but you're not going to talk to her like that. What do you need?"

Julian backed away. "Did you know?"

"God, Julian, you're like a dog with a bone. Yes, I knew."

I looked at Blake, confused. How did he know? Had Isaac told him?

"And you did it anyway?"

Blake scoffed. "You're kidding, right?"

I pulled out my desk chair and looked at the two of them. "I have work to do."

"I'm sure. There's another Steele brother for you to mount."

Blake smacked his brother in the back of the head and growled. "Fuck off with that, Julian."

I jabbed my finger into Julian's chest. "You're an asshole. And unless you have another brother, I've already mounted the three of you, and let me tell you, you weren't in the top two."

Blake snorted. "Damn."

I pushed past Julian and grabbed my purse. "I'm taking an early lunch."

CHAPTER FOURTEEN

Blake called to check on me after I left and told me that Julian was staying around, so I could take the afternoon off. Any other time, I would've insisted on going back to work, but I just wanted to hold Hank and pretend like nothing was happening in my world. I picked him up from Kara's office and took him home to give him plenty of attention.

We played on the living room floor for hours, had an early dinner and bath, and then settled in to watch Casey and Taylor play on the swing outside while we picked at the grass. Tyler was at a doctor's appointment and Kara got home from work late, so it was just me and the kids hanging out for a while. When Kara did get home, she showed up with a pizza and fed us all on the back porch. It was a nice quiet evening that made me almost believe I'd imagined everything that had happened.

I eventually settled on the couch with Hank in my arms and talked with Kara. She was exhausted from a long day of worrying about Tyler's doctor appointment and seemed to need a distraction.

"So, you stayed over at Isaac's for a while last night."

I groaned. "Let's not have this conversation."

"No, we should have it. I still want all the details."

"Do you think I'm horrible for leaving Hank here at night and going out?"

Scoffing, she shook her head. "No way. I think you're having your needs met, and you can't do that with Hank there. He's sleeping and doesn't even realize you're gone."

I sighed. "I still worry, you know? I'm being selfish."

"No, you're not. You've been consumed with taking care of him by yourself for a year. Now, you have help. You get to live your life now. If you weren't going over to Isaac's and letting him bone you, I'd be worried."

"Bone? Really?"

"Yeah, bone. What? Is that not a cool word anymore?" She looked up and grinned when she saw Tyler standing in the doorway. "Is bone not a cool word?"

He came in and held his hand out for hers. When she took it, he pulled her up and into his arms. "Sorry, Mal, we've got business. The kids are locked in their bedrooms for the night, and you've got Hank. We've got to go talk about boning."

"Ew."

Kara kissed Hank's head. "See you tomorrow, I guess."

Before they could slip away, the doorbell rang. I looked back at the door, even as Kara giggled and hurried towards it to answer it. My stomach fluttered with nerves as I found myself hoping it was Isaac or Blake. I stood up so I could see who was at the door, but I could've saved myself the trouble. Before I saw anything, Kara was already yelling for me.

"You're a wanted woman, Mal." Her voice was tinged with confusion, and I saw why as soon as I got closer.

Balancing Hank on my hip, I looked out and saw both Isaac *and* Blake. I felt my face go hot and found myself flustered beyond words. There were the two men who'd both been in me at the same time the night before, standing on my sister's doorstep.

"We came to check in." Blake took in Hank and grinned. "This is Hank, huh?"

Hank reached for Isaac as soon as he saw him and then looked at Blake and reached for him. I grinned at his response to them and handed him off to Blake. "This is Hank. He's heavy."

"How weak do you think I am?" He took Hank and tucked him into his chest, eyes instantly going soft. "Man, he's cute."

"So, you're just checking in on my little sister? Both of you?"

Isaac nodded. "Just checking in. And seeing if she and Hank want to come over to watch a movie."

I narrowed my eyes at him. He was really trying to ease me into dating them. Or him. I wasn't sure.

Tyler appeared from behind me. "I packed Hank's bag. Here you go."

Isaac took the bag and laughed. "Thanks."

"You packed his bag? You're just sending us away?" I hid a grin as I pretended to glare at Tyler. "Just the first man, or men, who come knocking get us?"

Tyler pulled Kara into his arms. "We have plans."

"Looks like you have to come over now. You're being kicked out." Blake bounced a happy Hank. "Plus, I've got the kid."

Kara kicked me in the butt, pushing me out the door. "Bye! Have a lovely night, you three."

"I need—" It didn't matter what I needed. The door was already shut behind me. Sighing, I turned to Blake and Isaac and put my hands on my hips. "What the hell?"

Isaac pulled me into his arms and kissed me. "We're dating, so we came over to check in."

"I don't date."

Blake leaned in and kissed the side of my head. "I told him about Julian. We wanted to see how you were feeling. Also, we wanted to see you."

I pulled away from them and talked to them over my shoulder as I went to get Hank's car seat. "You two are about as subtle as a rocket to the face."

"Subtle isn't our thing; you're right. We're much more into sharing and pleasing."

Isaac grunted. "Lots of sharing and pleasing."

I got edged out of the way as he took over grabbing the car seat and taking it to his truck. I snuck in under his arm to hook the seat in and turned around, still pressed against him, and tilted my head to look up at him. "I bet you didn't plan on getting a mom and her kid tonight."

He cupped my face in his hands and kissed me softly. When he pulled back, his eyes were happy. "Guess we just got lucky."

Blake handed me a slobbering Hank, and they both stood back and watched as I strapped him into his seat and adjusted the straps over his chest. Both men were quiet as they looked on, and when I looked back at them, they looked almost studious.

I climbed into the backseat next to Hank and took his bag from Isaac. Smiling out at them, I raised my brows. "Coming?"

They drove to the ranch in silence; the only sound filling the truck was a soft rock song on the radio and Hank trying his best to talk to me. When we parked, I took him out and carried him inside, wondering how he was going to fit into Isaac's house.

To my complete surprise, I watched as both men went around the house, preparing it for Hank. Things were moved and hidden, the TV was turned to cartoons, and Isaac even did a quick sweep before putting a blanket on the floor.

Noticing my mouth was hanging open, Isaac shrugged. "He has to be safe."

My chest tightened at watching the two of them take precautions for my son. It made me melt a little more than I should've, but I couldn't help it. They were sweet men, from what I'd seen so far, and when I was dating, sweet men weren't typically the men I found.

I sank onto the blanket with Hank and pulled his favorite little stuffed toy from his bag. "Thank you."

Blake settled across from me and chuckled when Hank instantly crawled to him. When Hank pulled himself up on Blake's strong thigh and bounced his little butt to the music playing on the TV, I watched Blake's heart swoon. His eyes went soft as Hank took his fingers to stabilize himself. "God, he's a beautiful baby."

I bit my lip and leaned back against the couch. I was playing with fire, bringing Hank around them, especially with Julian hanging around. I needed to gather some dignity and self-control and leave them alone.

"Have you eaten?" Isaac stroked my hair away from my face and smiled down at me. "I'm going to throw something together."

I leaned into his caress and found myself longing for more of his touch. "I ate earlier. I'd take something sweet if you have it, though."

He leaned down and pressed his lips to mine. "I'll figure it out."

I sighed happily and turned back to find Blake holding Hank and smiling at me. "What?"

"I think you like us."

I frowned. "We're not dating. Also, of course I like you. Enough, anyway."

He laughed, but it quickly turned into a groan as Hank leaned down to chew on his fingers. A string of slobber hung down from his hand and he shook his head at me when he noticed me laughing at him. "You taught him this, didn't you?"

"It's all natural."

"How does he produce this much liquid? He's making a puddle."

Still laughing, I grabbed a wipe from the diaper bag and crawled over to them, to Hank's pleasure. He started chewing faster on Blake's fingers, making even more drool. "Okay, little man. That's enough of that."

Blake reached over and kissed me, his warm lips moving over mine softly until I let out another little sigh of happiness and smiled. "You're so beautiful, Mal. It sucked not seeing you at your desk today."

"I won't make a habit of taking time off like that. I would've fought you more on it, but I was happy to get an afternoon with this little man."

"It's fine. It gave Hannah a chance to build her pile back."

My jaw dropped and a wave of frustration built in me. "Are you kidding me?"

He laughed and nodded. "Yeah, I am."

I finished wiping up Hank's drool and stayed there, close to them. Hank grabbed the end of my hair and played with it, a yawn erupting from his little body. "He won't make it much longer. We played a lot today."

"You could bring him to the office if you wanted. I'm sure you miss him." He grunted. "And it might actually give Hannah something to do. She loves kids."

"It wouldn't be a problem?"

"Of course not. Vicki already has plans to bring her kid to work with her, too. Although, I don't think Hannah will enjoy that kid as much. She's convinced that Vicki is the devil."

I grinned and leaned into his side. "I'd really like that. To try it, anyway. He's usually a pretty good baby, but he has his days."

Blake cradled Hank to his chest and gently rocked him. "Seems like a perfect baby to me."

Isaac came back in and settled against the couch. "Come here, Mal."

I raised my eyebrows at him.

"Please."

Smiling, I closed the distance between us and let him pull me between his thighs. Sitting with my back against his chest, I enjoyed my time with them. Hank fell fast asleep in Blake's arms, but Blake still held him. Isaac held me, nearly rocking *me* to sleep. It was nice to talk to them and listen to them talk to each other.

There was the elephant in the room, Julian, but no one brought him up. Not until the sound of a motorcycle coming up the drive sounded outside. I stiffened against Isaac and he wrapped his arms around me and pressed his lips to my ear.

"If he's rude to you, we'll just murder him and bury him out back."

I tried to laugh, but I was panicking. He was going to see Hank. He probably wouldn't realize anything, but he wasn't supposed to see the son we'd made together. He was never supposed to see him. "I think I should go home."

CHAPTER FIFTEEN

Isaac kissed the side of my head. "I'll take you home if you want. It might be better to work shit out with him now, though. He typically stays around for a few weeks when he comes down from the mountain. You might be seeing a lot of him around the office."

I groaned and dropped my head back on his chest. "Well, that sucks."

Blake looked at Isaac and nodded to the sleeping baby in his arms. "Don't let him come in here stomping around. Hank just fell asleep."

I grinned despite myself and crawled back to their sides to press a kiss to both of their cheeks. Blake took advantage of his and moved his head so I kissed his lips. Standing up, I sighed and then straightened my back. "Maybe I'll just talk to him on the porch. That way, if he shouts at me for trying to climb the Steele brothers' ladder of erections, he won't wake Hank."

Isaac laughed and stood up. "I'll come with you."

"I'm okay. I can handle him." At least I hoped I could.

He grunted and walked me to the door. "Was whatever happened between the two of you that bad?"

I cut my eyes to Hank without meaning to and shook my head. "It was barely anything. Sex behind the bar in town. Not that sex is barely anything. I just mean we barely spoke. God, that sounds terrible, too. I'm not a complete slut. Although, from what the two of you have experienced..."

Isaac bent to be eye level with me. "You're not a slut. There was nothing wrong with what we did together."

"Try telling your brother that."

"He knows there's nothing wrong with what we do." There was a tone to Isaac's voice that made me think he wasn't saying something, but then I heard heavy boots coming up the steps and didn't have time to press Isaac for more information.

Pushing him away, I slipped out the front door and came face to face with Julian. Face to chest, anyway. I tipped my head back, bumping it on the door, and stared into his annoyed face. Instead of giving in to his clear dislike of me and getting angry, I swallowed my nerves and forced a smile. "Hey. I thought maybe we could talk out here before we go in. That way, if you want to shout, you can do it out here."

Julian just stared at me for another few seconds before grumbling and heading over to one of the rockers.

"Although, I'm not sure why you'd want to shout at me." I sank into the rocker next to him and crossed my legs, suddenly realizing I was wearing a short sundress.

"So, what? You're just making yourself at home on the family ranch? You don't see how that might be weird?" His deep voice was even gruffer than normal and he didn't attempt to hide the mistrust and frustration in his eyes.

"I have a home, and it's not here. Your brothers picked me up from that home to hang out tonight." I sighed. "And I know it's weird. I know that everything about it is weird. Trust me when I tell you this isn't what I had in mind when I moved here."

"Am I interrupting whatever orgy you three were having?"

Shame washed over me, but I resisted showing him. "Yep. We've got a few other guys coming over soon, too, if you don't mind making this visit quick."

He snorted. "Tell me how you ended up finding the men in town who happen to have my same face."

I snorted right back at him. "Isaac's face is much more interesting than yours. And Blake's is just pretty."

That actually got a laugh. "Well, shit."

I looked out at the darkness that had engulfed the ranch. "I didn't mean to intrude on your life. It just happened. I was kind of hoping not to run into you for this exact reason. It's awkward."

"There goes my theory that you're some kind of deranged stalker, I guess."

"I barely have time to wash my hair some days. I can assure you that I don't have the time to stalk you."

"More meetings with your sister keeping you running around?"

I flushed at the memory of our first meeting and tugged at the hem of my dress. He remembered details of our meeting, which struck me as strange, but I ignored it. "If you want to talk with your brothers alone, I'll gladly go home. I just have to gather Hank and—"

Julian's eyes narrowed. "There's another man in there?"

I wagged my brows while standing. "Oh, yeah."

"What the fuck? Since when do they bring in another   "

"My son." I stopped at the door and turned back to face a too close Julian. "Hank is my son."

"You have a kid? Here?"

I opened the door and walked in to find Blake standing, still rocking Hank, and Isaac hovering around them. Biting my lip to keep from smiling at the sight, I walked closer and saw that Hank was awake and looked teary-eyed. "Did he wake up?"

"It's my fault. I tried to stand up without disturbing him, but I must've jostled him just enough to startle him. He woke up mad about it."

I gently took Hank and held him against my chest, patting his butt ever so lightly. "There we go, baby boy. You're okay. Momma's got you."

Isaac grunted. "That's all it took, huh? Nothing we did worked."

Blake frowned. "I think my feelings are hurt."

Laughing, I cradled the back of Hank's head and walked around the kitchen, noticing there was ice cream out on the counter, next to a couple of big sandwiches. I pointed at the ice cream and looked over at Isaac. "Mine?"

He nodded and handed me a spoon while he scooped a big bowl full of the chocolate goodness. "So. You two good?"

I shoved a spoonful of ice cream into my mouth between patting Hank and glanced back at Julian, who's gone non-verbal. Shrugging, I looked away and tried to ignore the fact that Hank and his father were in the same room. My hands shook, but I tried to hide it by shoveling more ice cream into my mouth.

"Julian? You good?"

"So. The three of you are just hanging out...with a baby?" Shaking his head, Julian scratched his beard. "How old is the kid?"

I dropped my spoon and winced when Hank let out a loud wail. "Sorry, sorry."

Isaac cleaned up my mess while Blake rubbed Hank's little back. "What's wrong, little guy?"

"He didn't nap today, so he's cranky. It's my fault. I kept him up to spend time with him. I can just go." I looked around frantically for his bag, even as he started crying louder. "I'm sorry."

Isaac caught me and pulled me into his arms. "Slow down. He's okay. Unless you just want to go home, we can handle him letting us know he's angry for a bit."

I blinked back overwhelmed tears and kept my head planted in his chest. "He'll stop soon. He's just exhausted."

"He'll stop when he's done and then I'll pour you something to drink to go with your ice cream. How does that sound?"

I nodded and pulled away. "I'm just going to get him settled on your bed."

Hank calmed down pretty much once we were in the dark bedroom. I rocked him and sang him the lullaby that Kara had sung to me when I was little. In under a minute, he was passed out again, his little thumb shoved into his mouth.

"You've got a pretty voice." Julian's low tone came from right behind me, and I jumped. "Sorry. Didn't mean to scare you."

I shook my head. "You're fine. Help me make a pillow wall around him?"

My brain screamed at me that what I was doing was weird. Having Julian help with Hank was wrong when he didn't know. It was wrong that he didn't know. It was wrong that I was there with them in the first place. Everything I was doing was wrong.

Julian stayed quiet as he helped me arrange pillows around Hank. He sat on the bed across from me and stared at Hank. "He's cute."

I sank down next to Hank and looked him over. He was more than cute. He was perfect. While he was sleeping, it was harder to see Julian in him, but when his eyes were open, the pale blue color gave it away. To me, anyway. "I'm just going to stay with him for a bit to make sure he stays asleep."

He studied Hank for a moment more and then left me there, silently worrying about what he saw when he looked at our son. I was so scared of what he'd do if he knew. How much of Hank would he want? How much could I share without dying a little?

I laid down next to Hank and fought the urge to scoop him up and run. It wasn't easy. Closing my eyes and holding his little hand in mine, I told myself I'd stay there for a few minutes and then go back out to talk to the guys.

The next thing I knew, I was waking up to pee. Without recognizing that I wasn't in my own bed, I checked on Hank and then went to the bathroom. It wasn't until I was washing my hands that I realized I wasn't at Kara's house. I found my reflection looking back at me, looking tired and rumpled. I pulled my hair into a bun and wiped smudged mascara from under my eyes before going out to find the guys.

I found them asleep on the couches in the living room. Isaac and Blake. I didn't see Julian. I instantly felt so guilty, seeing their big bodies folded awkwardly to fit on a couch too small for them. I grabbed the heavy quilt from the back of the couch and draped it over Isaac before taking the blanket from the floor and shaking it out. Covering Blake with it, I stepped back and rubbed my face. Things were weird.

I liked them. I didn't know how I liked them when I'd barely known them and I'd barely spent any time with them, but I did. They seemed like good guys. I was in over my head, though. I wasn't someone who could balance having sex with multiple men. I was barely able to make it to the grocery store while raising a kid, much less balance relationships.

A creak sounded from the front porch and I realized the door was open. Walking towards it, I peeked out and saw Julian's long body stretched out in one of the rockers.

I stepped out as quietly as I could and looked him over. In sleep, his face was void of all the harshness. He actually looked sweet. I found myself thinking of him again, the same way he'd snuck into my mind during my pregnancy. The daydreams of what it would've been like to have him there, they were kryptonite. I shook my head and went to step away, but Julian suddenly caught my wrist.

"Not polite to stare."

I swallowed down all the softness I'd been feeling and gently pulled away from him. "You're going to catch a cold out here. You should come in."

"The mother thing really grew on you, huh?"

I rolled my eyes and shook my head. "Just worried the orgies will stop if your brothers are busy taking care of you."

He snorted out a laugh and pulled himself up to his full height. "You don't know my brothers. Or the power of male arousal. It works through anything."

"I can sleep somewhere else with Hank if you want Isaac's bed."

"I'm not staying. I was just waiting around for...I don't know, I guess." He sighed and looked out into the darkness. "I'll see you tomorrow, Red."

Chapter Sixteen

When I came in the next morning, Kara's face was barely being held together with all the nosiness she was experiencing. She looked demented when she passed Hank off to Tyler and dragged me up to my room.

"He's coming to work with me today!"

Tyler grumbled and continued eating his pancakes.

"Tell me everything. Right now. Why did two of the Steele brothers show up to pick you up? What happened? I can't believe you spent the night with them. What'd you do? Where'd Hank sleep?"

I grabbed her shoulders and shook her. "Breathe, woman!"

She followed me into the bathroom as I turned on the hot water and started undressing. "I need to know what is going on with you. Is it Isaac you're with? Or Blake? Or...both?"

I stripped down to my birthday suit, used to being forced into getting ready in front of her. "Kara—"

"Oh, my god!" She leaned into me and started poking and prodding different spots. "You have hickeys! You little slut!"

I slapped her hands away, embarrassed at her teasing. "Shut up. Don't touch my boobs!"

She poked it again and threw her head back, laughing. "You had sex. And a lot of it, from the looks of things."

"Get out. You're banned from my bathroom!" I pushed her out, all while she was still poking at my body and laughing. When I got her past the threshold, I closed the door and locked it. "You can't get gossip until you learn personal boundaries!"

When I was clean and dressed, I found Tyler playing with Hank in the living room. He looked up at me and laughed. "Your sister is about to explode with curiosity. She left for work with two different shoes on, she was so distracted."

"You didn't tell her, did you?"

He snorted. "Hell no. I just want to watch the world burn."

I laughed and grabbed a banana to shove down before grabbing Hank and getting everything ready to take him to work with me. By the time I got to work, I was the last one in the building, it seemed. Hannah was already in her chair, next to Julian, talking about who knew what, Blake was leaning against my desk, and Isaac was sitting in my chair.

They all looked up at me, and I had to take a step back at having all of them focused on me so early. "What? I'm not late."

Blake laughed and came over to take Hank from me. "You're not late. We were thinking of ordering breakfast in today. Want something?"

I thought of the banana I'd eaten and slowly nodded. "Donuts."

Isaac pulled me in for a hug and pressed a kiss to the top of my head. "Dates in the morning count as dating, too."

I found myself smiling and pushing him away. "Just bring me donuts and we can talk about the rest later."

Hannah was already taking Hank into her arms. He seemed enamored by the color of her hair and wasted no time in trying to grab it. "Oh, my god. I had no clue you were hiding the cutest baby ever from me."

"I'll be back with breakfast." Isaac patted my ass as he walked by, his eyes heated. "I like this dress."

Blake's phone rang and he cupped my chin in his hand before pressing a kiss to my mouth and backing away. "Be right back."

Hannah was already on the floor with Hank, entertaining him by making all kinds of sounds and motions. He seemed like he was in heaven with his new favorite show.

That left Julian. He watched me quietly as I put my bags down and sank into my chair. I powered up my computer and then slowly looked back at him, finding him still watching me.

"Why do I feel like I failed some kind of Julian test already?"

He stretched out in his chair, his long legs invading my space. "No tests or failures. I'm just thinking."

I took my foot and pushed his foot out of my way. "Why does that seem scarier than a test?"

"You look different."

I narrowed my eyes at him. "If you're about to tell me that I'm chunkier than I was back then, I'll send you through this window."

He pulled his chair closer and shook his head. "You know you're just as beautiful now as you were then. Maybe even prettier. You just look different. There's a softness to you that wasn't there before."

"So, it *is* about my weight?"

He laughed and scooted away again. "Not even a little bit."

I looked over at Hannah and Hank and then back to Julian. "I'm sorry if this is awkward for you."

He gave me a panty-melting smile that packed enough of a punch that I felt it in the eggs forming in my uterus. "Not awkward at all."

Flustered, I turned back to my computer and bit back a groan when it took me multiple times to get logged in. My brain short-circuited and I was caught in a moment of panic, wondering if I should just open a game of Hearts.

"What made you move here?"

I glanced back at Julian and bit my lip. "Not you, if that's what you're getting at."

He laughed. "It's just a question, Red."

I narrowed my eyes at him. "I came to be closer to my sister."

"How'd you end up here? In this office?"

"Kara, my sister, told me about it." I turned to face him completely and watched as he looked away from my legs. "Is this my second job interview?"

He stared at me for a while before sighing and shifting back to his corner. "Nope. Just making small talk."

"You suck at small talk."

He chuckled and shrugged. "Don't like it much, to tell you the truth. Don't do it a lot, either."

"Julie lives in a cabin on the mountain, all alone." Hannah made a face like she hadn't meant to reveal she'd been listening in.

I couldn't help the giggle that escaped. "Julie?"

Scowl firmly back in place, Julian stood up and pointed at Hannah. "You're a traitor. That's a secret name."

"Aw, Julie, don't be like that." I caught his wrist the same way he had mine the night before. "No need to run from a sweet little name."

His forefinger lightly stroked my hand as he looked down at me. "I'm not running, Red. Just grabbing a coffee. Want something?"

It felt like a trap, but coffee sounded good. "A coffee would be amazing."

"Say please."

Instantly, I was taken back to his truck and having to beg him to fuck me. My face heated and I bit my tongue hard to stop from just giving into him. What was wrong with me? I met his gaze and saw the hunger there, so clear and strong. Was he thinking about the same thing? Did he remember?

I bit my lip and retreated. I couldn't afford to get involved with him. It was dangerous enough that I was around him with Hank at all. "I'll just get it myself."

He braced his hand in front of me on my desk and leaned down until he could whisper into my ear. "That's too bad. I really liked the way you beg."

I shoved away from my desk, the wheels on my chair sending me sliding into the desk behind me. I popped out of my chair and retreated even farther from Julian. He was dangerous. Just like with his brothers, there was an animal magnetism that drew me in, but I couldn't afford to take the chance with him. I couldn't afford to take the chance with any of them.

"Suit yourself." He backed away and looked down at Hannah. "Coffee, Han?"

"Sure, I'll—"

"Get it yourself, traitor." With the teasing laugh only a cousin could hit another cousin with, he walked off to the kitchen and left the air in the room a little cooler.

"Julie seems to like you." Hannah looked back at me and smiled. "They all do. I haven't seen Isaac show up here in forever."

I pulled my chair back to my desk and sank into it, feeling heavier than I did before I knew Julian remembered juicy details from our time together. "I don't date."

Laughing, Hannah kept right on playing with Hank. "Sure. It's just that my mom's house sits close enough to the front drive of the ranch that we pretty much see everyone coming and going."

My face paled. "What?"

"Relax, Mallory. Everyone knows the triplets do things a little differently. Plus, you're a modern woman. If anyone judges you, they're assholes. A woman is allowed to do with her body whatever she wants."

"What do you mean everyone knows?"

"The triplets have lived in this town since they were born. They've done everything here. People notice things. Like how they sometimes act like one man, instead of three. Although, it's been a long time since that's happened, according to my mom."

"Everyone knows?"

"Yeah, it's not a big deal."

Not a big deal. "Everyone in your family?"

"Everyone in town, Mallory. That's why it's not a big deal. The triplets just live a little differently than most people. My mom said that if anyone ever judges them, there's a whole line of people here willing to vouch for them. And do some ass-kicking."

Everyone in town knew that I was having sex with multiple men at once. Is that what she was saying? Did my sister? Did Tyler and the kids? Did Berna at the diner? I was going to have a heart attack, I was pretty sure. Everyone knew.

CHAPTER SEVENTEEN

"Mallory?"

I hadn't even realized I was standing, but I was, and then Isaac was coming in, looking at me with wide eyes and a handful of donut boxes. I looked at Hannah and pointed at Hank. "Can you watch him? I just need a minute."

"Of course."

I grabbed one of the boxes of donuts on the way to the bathroom and locked myself in with it. I knocked the toilet lid down and sat down, head between my knees. Everyone knew. Everyone. Knew.

I groaned and sat back up. The head between the knees thing wasn't working. Instead, I opened the donut box and grabbed one. Shoving half of it in my mouth at once, I let out a little scream and looked up at the ceiling, like there would be answers there.

"Mal?" Blake's voice was gentle as he called to me. "What's wrong?"

"Whath's wrongth?" I chewed my donut and tried again. "What's wrong? What's wrong is that everyone knows!"

"Everyone knows what?" Julian joined Blake at the door.

Isaac was right there with his brothers. "Apparently, Cousin Hannah, or the girl we used to know as our cousin, told Mallory that everyone knows about this."

"This?" Julian grunted. "Oh. *This*."

"Yeah, *this*! The whole town knows I'm letting multiple brothers do things to me! *Sexual* things!" I grabbed a second donut and shoved it into my mouth. "Thethual thingsth!"

"Well, this is a code red and I'm not equipped for it. I haven't been a part of this whole tryst just yet, so I didn't do this. I didn't break her; I'm not fixing her."

I jerked the door open and glared at Julian while wiping my mouth. "Yet? Yet? If you ever think you're putting your thing back in me, you've got another thing coming! I'm done with the three of you! You let me do this, knowing I was going to be the talk of the town because of it. People probably think you're putting your things in my butt! Just a dick everywhere. Here a dick, there a dick, everywhere a dick, dick!"

Blake covered his mouth and looked away.

"Are you laughing? Are you actually laughing right now?" I shoved the box of donuts at him and stomped towards the front of the office. I knew I didn't want to scare Hank, so I stomped into Blake's office and slammed the door behind me. Then, I realized I needed more donuts, so I opened the door just as the three idiots were trying to get in. "Give me those back, you giant, walking turd."

One of them put their foot in the way of me closing the door, and they all three filed in after me. They stood in a small semi-circle, watching me like I was a feral cat, primed and ready to rip their faces off. Maybe I was.

"We know you're upset, Mal, but let us talk to you and explain."

I frowned at Isaac, the least mad at him because he'd brought donuts and hadn't said anything too stupid so far. I took a bite of a donut with cream in it and pouted when the cream plopped out on my dress. I realized I was going to cry about a half-second before I was crying. I rubbed at the cream and dropped the donut on Blake's desk, sinking into his chair. "I'm a mess and everyone is going to think this is like *the dress*. You know? And that other dress didn't end too well for her. Monica still gets shit on."

Isaac hurried around the desk to kneel next to me. "Hey, I promise no one is thinking poorly of you."

"And if anyone ever did, we'd murder them."

I wiped my eyes and tilted my head at Julian. "Murder them?"

He wagged his brows. "Anything for the girl who will never sleep with me, or any of us, again."

A smile played at my lips, but I bit it back. "I'm a mom. I'm already judged for what I do. In the city, if I worked too much, I was an absentee mom who sucked. If I worked too little, I was setting a bad example for my kid. If people thought I was dating, they judged me. If they thought I was keeping Hank away from men, they judged me. It was nonstop, and now I get a new start, and everyone knows I'm sleeping with multiple men at the same time!"

"It's not weird here for us. Everyone knows us. They know all about us." Blake gestured around the office. "This town has been supportive of us from the very beginning. They take care of us. They're not going to judge you."

"You're men. I'm not the same. I'm a woman and a mom. It's harder. They're going to think I'm a slut. They're going to think I'm a bad mom." I angrily swiped at my eyes as the tears kept coming. "I'm not a bad mom. I'm a good mom. And I'm not usually a slut. I haven't slept with anyone in forever before y'all. And even if I had, that's my choice. But people don't see it that way."

"You're not a slut, Mal. You're in a relationship with us. This is a consensual thing that's happening between adults. People know that."

"A relationship?"

Julian grunted. "I guess this is my cue to go."

Blake shook his head. "No. You, too. You're a part of us, Julian, whether you like it or not. We come together."

I giggled, the stress breaking my brain a little. "Yeah, you do."

"What I mean is that we're a package deal. The three of us go together when we go. That was always the plan, Julian."

Isaac nodded. "That's why we called you down. We wanted to do this right. With you."

I wasn't as amused anymore. I stood up and crossed my arms over my chest. "What the hell? Were you ever going to involve me in this?"

"She clearly doesn't want to be with me. I'm not doing this shit again." Julian's voice was thick with anger as he backed away. "You couldn't pay me enough to make me want to do this."

"Julie, just wait a fucking second." Isaac turned to me and took my face in his hands. "All of this comes down to you. What you want, when you want it. This wasn't supposed to all happen so fast, but here it is. We want to be with you. The three of us. In a relationship. With dating."

"And lots of sex with maybe some butt stuff." Blake grinned at me and then shrugged when Isaac hit him. "Just saying."

"How does that even work? I've never been good at a relationship with one guy, much less three. And I'm still mad at all of you."

Julian backed away even more. "This isn't how it works. When you force someone to be with all three of us, when they don't want all three of us, it doesn't end well. Look at us. We barely made it through the last time. I'm not doing it again."

Watching the crack in their relationship seem to grow and split open in front of me, I felt my own chest ache. I didn't know what I was doing, but I didn't want Julian to leave. There were all the reasons in the world, and in the next room, for me to let him go, but I couldn't do it. "Julian. Wait. I don't want you to go."

Isaac sank into the chair I'd vacated and sighed. "Thank Christ."

Julian rested his hands on his hips and glared at me. "You're just saying that."

"I'm too angry at the three of you to convince you that I want you here right now. I don't feel like saying nice things. And I'm not talking about any relationship. I just want to sit here and eat my donuts while figuring out how I'm going to face my sister over dinner tonight, knowing that she knows that I'm getting railed by more than one man at a time."

Blake grinned again. "And doing butt stuff."

"I'm going to murder you, Blake. I don't need this job that badly. I will murder you and leave you here for Hannah to clean up."

He pulled me into his arms and grunted as I elbowed his side. "Ouch."

Being passed off, I found myself standing in front of Julian, our eyes moving questionably over each other. It was clear that neither of us knew if we could trust the other and as my anger settled, I found myself wanting to know what'd happened to him.

He looked down at me and gently rested his hands on my waist. "Are you sure?"

I laughed a little and shrugged. "I don't know what I'm doing. I'm officially the woman in town sleeping with a set of triplets and I feel like an embarrassment, but I also remember how it felt to kiss you."

He swore and pulled me into his chest. "I swear to god, if you're just doing this because you think this is what we want, I'm going to help you murder my brothers."

I could hear the pain in his voice and I didn't like it. I almost preferred him being an asshole. I stroked my hand over his cheek and smiled up at him. "I don't do anything just because someone wants me to, or because someone thinks I should."

He sighed and leaned down to plant a hard kiss on my mouth before pulling away. "I've got shit to do today."

He left the door open after him, and Isaac walked by me after, his kiss longer lasting and deeper. "You suck at not dating."

Blake pulled me into his chest and grunted. "So bad. You're the worst at not dating I've ever seen anyone be."

"I hate you both." I looked over at the donuts longingly and sighed. "I need those donuts and like half an hour alone."

"Here. You stay and we'll go."

I looked out at Hank and shook my head. "I'm going to take a walk with him instead. I need to think."

After prying Hank away from Hannah and forcing Isaac and Blake to stop watching me from the doorway, I took a walk around the front of the business. I stayed far away from the lumberyard and the road, making sure to keep Hank safe and away from the sawdust. He happily tugged at my hair and played with my face, so untouched by the world around him. He didn't have a care in the world. I wanted to keep him that way.

I knew the world would touch him eventually and he'd have to learn that things weren't always easy, but I was going to do everything I could to make sure he had a real childhood. That meant my choices had to align with what he needed for that to happen. The only thing was...I didn't know what that took.

Kara had basically raised me herself while our parents did only god knew what. There wasn't a lot of childhood to be had for either of us. I was ill-equipped to give Hank everything he needed, and suddenly, his mother was the woman in town banging the triplets. One of whom happened to be his father.

Julian was another huge source of worry. I didn't want to hurt him. It seemed like someone had already done that. I couldn't chance bringing him into Hank's life as a father, though. I didn't think I could, at least. Julian didn't seem stable. What if he got angry at me and took Hank? What if he ruined everything I was trying to do with Hank?

Another voice in my head spoke up. What if he was what Hank needed? What if he needed Hank?

Kissing Hank's cheeks, I sighed. I would have to decide sooner rather than later. I couldn't chance hurting the guys, if that was even something that was possible. For all I knew, it was all sexual with them. I just couldn't string it out.

CHAPTER EIGHTEEN

"Are you fucking kidding me?" Kara stared out the kitchen window with her mouth hanging open. "They're all here! They're all here, Tyler!"

"Swear jar, Mom!" Casey screeched as she ran into the living room to get the swear jar and was cut off by Taylor last minute. "Taylor! I was going to get it!"

Tyler hurried to the window and actually cackled. "Well. That didn't take any time. Looks like Mallory is a star."

A wave of dread washed over me. They were not all three showing up at my sister's house. I would kill them. I shifted Hank higher on my hip and tried to wipe the baby food off my hands. "What is it?"

Kara clapped her hands and hurried to the front door. "I am never going to get over this. You are going to spend the rest of your life telling me all the details."

I looked at Tyler and sighed. "It's the brothers, isn't it?"

"Yep. Looks like they cleaned up, too." He looked me over and shook his head. "You didn't even try, did you?"

I narrowed my eyes at him and looked down at myself. I was still in my work dress, but I had baby food all over me. Hank was just smearing it everywhere. "I need a towel."

"Well, hello, Steele brothers. Are you here for my beautiful sister?" Kara immediately invited them in and turned a massive smile on me. "I was just going to take Hank from you. He needs a bath and bed, and I've missed the little booger today."

On cue, Hank reached for his Aunt Kara and left me standing in front of all three brothers and Tyler, covered in goo and unsure if I was going to die of embarrassment or kill them all first.

Tyler snorted. "Man, this is something. Should I get my camera and take a picture of the first official date?"

"I don't date!" Glaring at Tyler, I grabbed his arm and pulled him away. "If you'll just excuse us for one second."

Tyler laughed when I dragged him out of the entryway and into the living room. "What? This is too good."

I pushed him towards the couch and pointed at him. "Stay. I mean it."

In the entryway, Blake was laughing when I got back. "I told them you were going to be pissed about this."

Isaac grunted. "He didn't."

Julian moved closer and scooped a splatter of baby food from my neck before bringing his finger to his mouth and tasting it. "Bananas. Pretty good."

My blood heated and I stood there, staring up at him with my mouth hanging open. I wanted him to do it again, but with his tongue directly on my skin. "I need to change before... I should change before we go. If we're going."

Isaac walked by us and patted Julian on the shoulder. "I'll wait in the living room with Tyler."

"Me too." Blake leaned in and kissed me quickly before backing away from us. "Take your time getting changed."

I didn't mean to take Julian's hand and pull him after me, but I did. Upstairs in my room, I pushed the door closed behind us and locked it. Leaning against it, I debated for a second if I should pounce on him, but he was already moving.

Grabbing my ass and scooping me into his arms, Julian slid his mouth over mine. Spinning us around, he walked me over to my bed and dropped me on top of it. "Panties off."

I yanked them down while my brain struggled to keep up. "Bad idea, right? This is bad."

He spread my legs and buried his face between my thighs, instantly finding my clit and sucking. Dragging my ass closer to the bed, he hooked my legs over his shoulders and growled into my core.

I cried out before I could contain my pleasure and moaned when Julian reached up and covered my mouth with his hand. Working my hips against his mouth, I grabbed at his hair and came so fast that I nearly bucked him off of me. The feeling of his laughter against my sensitive bud made me moan into his hand.

"Jesus, Red." He lifted his mouth and looked up at me, his eyes brighter than I'd seen them since he'd shown up again. "Fucking wildcat."

I bit my lip and reached for him, hungry for more, despite common sense telling me it was a bad idea.

Julian easily grabbed me and spun me around so my back was against his chest. Holding my arms against my sides, he growled into my ear and nipped it. "I don't think you want the whole house hearing you get fucked right now, Red. From what I remember, you're not quiet when I fuck you."

I rubbed my bare ass against his jeans and groaned. "I could be quiet."

He bent me forward on the bed and surprised me by slapping my ass. The stinging shocked me, but it also heightened my need. Looking back at him over my shoulder, I found him staring down at me with heat in his eyes. "Get changed. If I take you here and now, the whole house is going to know it. And while you might like my brothers hearing, and even coming to join, I don't think you want your sister to know what you sound like when you come."

I stood up and yanked my dress down. "Fine."

He smiled. "You mad, Red?"

I hurried into my closet and searched for a dress. "No. I'm horny and I think my brain is broken. Why the hell do I want this so desperately?"

"If you asked my brothers, they'd tell you some shit about it just being right."

I paused. "And you? What would you tell me?"

"Well, Red, I wouldn't tell you anything." He leaned into the closet and met my gaze. "Not for a while anyway."

I frowned even as I grabbed a dress and pulled it down. "Why not?"

He stepped into the small space with me and reached behind me to unzip my dress. Slowly pulling it down, he undressed me patiently and gently. By the time I stepped out of the dress, I was shaking with need. Julian ran his finger over my breast and nipple before looking up at my eyes and shrugging. "Maybe you'll find out someday."

I sighed as he helped me get dressed, his hands roaming as he did. The dress wasn't even zipped yet and he already had me pinned against the wall with his fingers in me. My mouth found his and I kissed him in a way that probably revealed too much. A year and nine months had passed since I'd kissed him that way, but the feelings were still there, wild and raw. I didn't know how or why, but they were. The same intense feelings I felt for Isaac and Blake when I kissed them.

I needed something to get my brain away from that feeling, so I sank to my knees between Julian and the wall and worked at his pants.

"Red, that's not necessary."

I looked up at him as I got his cock free and rubbed the tip of him over my lips. "It's necessary for me."

He swore and braced his hands on the wall above me as I opened my mouth and took him in. I'd had practice with the size of his brothers so I was more confident as I took him in deep and held him there, swallowing around his head at the entrance of my throat. "Goddamn, Red."

I moaned my approval and sucked harder while sliding him out and bobbing up and down on the head. Working him into my cheeks, I showed him the surely vulgar picture of his cock filling my mouth. Then I took him in until I gagged and listened as he swore my name over and over again. Feeling wild and bold, I reached up and cupped his balls, lightly tugging and massaging them while I did my best to swallow his entire shaft. I felt like something out of a porn, but there was a side of me that liked it.

Julian locked his hand in my hair and held my head back until just the tip of him was on my tongue. "You're going to make me come. Where do you want me, Red?"

I sucked him back in deep while holding his eye contact. His fingers bit into my scalp, and I breathed between thrusts of his hips, but I could see him losing himself as he came apart. With a deep growl, he shot his seed down the back of my throat. I swallowed everything he gave me and licked him clean before pulling back and fixing him back into his pants.

Julian pulled me up and kissed me hard before holding me against the wall and staring down at me. "You're going to end up stuck with us if you're not careful."

I licked my lips and shrugged like the idea didn't equally terrify and excite me. "I don't think I know how to be careful anymore."

Sinking his fingers into the flesh of my hips, he tilted his head back and groaned my name before moving away and holding his hands up. "I just need to wait outside or I'm going to fuck you right here and now. Politeness be damned."

I laughed and leaned against the doorframe as he crossed the room to leave. "So that was polite?"

With a dark look over his shoulder at me, Julian looked me over once more before grunting and leaving. All alone with the feeling of his beard still rough between my thighs and my jaw aching, I trailed into my bathroom and got cleaned up before finishing getting dressed and heading down to find Hank.

I walked in on Kara and Tyler sitting across from my three men, the kids sitting next to them, like some kind of freaky family feud. I made a choking sound and froze. "What's going on?"

Kara cackled as she looked at me. "Nothing. We're just getting to know your dates, Mal."

"Aunt Mal, I can't believe you get to kiss three boys and they don't get mad about it. Sarah Jamie at school kissed two boys once and they got so mad." Casey sighed. "I'm going to be just like you when I grow up."

Taylor scoffed. "Like you could even get one boyfriend."

Tyler shook his head. "No boyfriends until you're sixty-four. Then, if you want five boyfriends, you can have five."

Julian snorted. "Good luck finding three weirdos like us."

I waved my hands. "Okay, this is weird for me. We're going to go."

Kara smacked my hands away when I tried to take Hank from her. "He's mine tonight. I missed him so much today."

I sighed. "You're a lot."

"And you owe me a lot. Casey really needed to go up to get her iPad earlier, but I told her that the top floor of the house was off-limits while there was a boy up there."

I looked over to find Casey staring up at my three men, her eyes wide. "God, this is a mess."

Pulling me closer, she hugged me and snorted in my ear while trying to hold in a laugh. "Sorry, sorry. I just really love you and I can't wait to tie you to a chair and torture you until you tell me everything."

I took Hank from her and hugged him tight before kissing him goodbye. "Be good for Aunt Kara. Or shit on her bed. Whatever you feel like."

"Swear jar!" Casey managed to grab the jar before Taylor and stuck her tongue out at him. "Ten bucks, Aunt Mal."

I narrowed my eyes at her and grabbed my wallet from my purse. "I don't think I like this swear jar."

"I think it's necessary. Your Aunt Mal has a really dirty mouth." Julian said it so straight-faced that I almost could've believed that he wasn't being dirty until he looked at me and wagged his brows.

"And that's our cue! We'll be leaving now."

"We'll get her back before you leave for work in the morning." Isaac took my shoulders and guided me towards the front door. He cut off my objections with a slap on the ass that I hoped he knew he'd pay for later.

Chapter Nineteen

I rode next to Julian in the back and glared at the three of them. "You don't get to just sweep me away and decide when I'll come back."

Isaac apologized first. "You're right. We're sorry. We'll ask next time."

"Yeah, sorry. Do you want to stay the night with us?"

I scoffed at Blake. "That's beside the point."

Julian unbuckled his seatbelt and moved closer to me. "Is it?"

"What are you doing? I'm mad at the three of you right now."

"I was with you. I'm innocent." He undid my buckle and looked up at his brother. "Drive safe."

I gasped as he pulled me into his lap and spread my legs apart with his thighs. "What are you doing?"

Reaching around, he traced my lower lips over my panties and bit his lip. "I guess apologizing."

I meant to push him away, but as soon as my hands touched his chest, I ended up stroking up to his shoulders and down his arms. I loved how strong they all were.

Lowering his voice and holding his lips against my ear, he heightened my arousal even more. "And making my brothers jealous. They can see me touching you."

I shuddered as he slipped my panties to the side and ran just the tip of his finger through my folds. I pressed my forehead against his and moaned. "This is an acceptable apology."

"You rode my fingers once before, Red. Want to do it again while they watch? Let them hear how good it feels."

I gasped when he pushed two fingers into me and held them deep. It was dirty and felt so extreme to have Isaac and Blake watching, but I was lost in the sensations. I braced one arm on the seat in front of me, bumping Isaac as I did, and lifted myself just enough to come down on Julian's fingers hard. I dropped my head back and moaned as Julian grasped my breast through my dress.

"That's it, Red. Ride my fingers. Fuck yourself how you need it." Julian's voice was louder, making sure his brothers knew exactly what was happening.

I did just what he said. Using his fingers to throw myself towards another orgasm, I lost my grip on the seat and grabbed Isaac's shoulder instead. He let out a frustrated growl that spurred me on. I moaned louder and moved harder and faster.

"Do you want to come for me?"

"Yes!"

Clamping his arm around me, he held me down on his fingers and kissed me. "Say please, Red."

I cried out, need and frustration building. Locking my lips, I struggled against his hold, trying to push myself over the edge. I was so close.

"Don't be stubborn, Red. Just say please. Say it and I'll let you come." He growled against my neck. "Say it and I'll fuck you until you come."

"Please!"

Blake's deep chuckle was strained as he leaned over the seat and took my face in his hands. "You're fucking perfect."

I grabbed his face and kissed him while Julian lifted my hips and freed himself. He pulled back and watched my face as Julian lined our bodies up and pulled me down on his cock. My mouth fell open and I cried out as I was suddenly stuffed full.

Blake stroked my throat and pressed his lips to my ear. "Ride him, baby."

I realized I was still clutching desperately to Isaac and the feeling of all three of them being around me, wanting me, spurred me into an alternate version of myself. I felt sexy and powerful as I stared into Blake's hot eyes and started doing as he said. Lifting myself and sliding back down, I rolled my hips and moaned at the feeling of Julian's cock twitching in me.

"Fuck, Red. Do that again."

I grabbed his shoulder with my other hand and circled my hips, squeezing him as I did it. His swear urged me on, and I set a fast, dizzying pace. Riding Julian while Blake held my face and kissed me was intoxicating. Every forward thrust of my hips rubbed my clit just perfectly, and I was teetering on the edge in no time.

More hands ran over my breasts, undressing me. I moaned loudly, overwhelmed by the sensations. Hands found my bare breasts, fingers pinched and teased my nipples.

"Come for us, Mal." Isaac's voice was low in my other ear, his desire sounding almost painful.

Blake nipped my throat, his breathing rough as he watched me. "Fuck, baby. You were made for us."

Julian grabbed my hips and lifted me so he could drive his cock into me from below. Hard and fast, he pistoned into me, forcing a scream from my chest as a powerful orgasm hit me. He pulled me off of his shaft and lifted me until I was balanced awkwardly on the seat in front of him. Then, he covered my core with his mouth and worked through my orgasm and into a smaller one, drinking me in as he did.

Panting and feeling thoroughly fucked, I didn't argue as I was lifted into Isaac's arms and pulled out of the truck. I hadn't even realized we were at the ranch. Half-naked and still moaning, I was carried into the house and straight to the bed.

Isaac put me down and tried to move away, but I caught his arm and pulled him down with me. "You can rest, Mal."

I wrapped my leg around his waist and pressed into his rock-hard erection that strained against his jeans. "I don't want to rest. I feel like I'm never going to get enough."

He kissed me and trailed his mouth down to my breasts. Taking a nipple into his mouth, he nipped and growled when I gasped and arched my hips up to him. "Greedy little thing."

Blake settled on the bed at my feet, his shirt gone. "I like you greedy. Are you ready for us? For all of us?"

I nodded instantly, uninhibited by any of my normal hang-ups. "Yes, please."

Julian appeared on my other side and growled low in his throat. "That's it, Red. You know what you want, don't you?"

I reached for them, rubbing Isaac and Julian through their jeans while Blake spread my legs and buried his mouth between them. I threw my head back as he licked me in long strokes that left nothing untouched.

Julian yanked his shirt over his head and threw it across the room before unbuttoning his pants and shoving them off. I watched him undress and then watched as Isaac did the same. My head spun as Blake pushed me towards an orgasm and then backed off, slowly torturing me. I reached for his head, but Julian took my hand and shook his head.

"Let him have his fun."

I writhed as they took control of my body. My heart raced, and I panted as Blake took me almost to orgasm again and then stopped. When he lifted his face to look at me, it was wet, and his grin said he was having a great time. "I hate you."

He laughed and lowered his head again. His tongue centered at my back entrance and fucked me slowly. His fingers went to my core and he pushed in three fingers, curling them up to rub against a magical spot. I instantly clinched on his fingers and cried out.

Isaac knelt next to my head and swore when I grabbed him and pulled him closer so I could take him into my mouth. Taking him in deep, I moaned when fingers circled over my clit. I reached for Julian even as I found myself hurtling into outer space on an orgasm that felt like it'd kill me. My body tightened painfully and then burst free all at once. Everything went dark for a second and lights flashed behind my eyes as I came harder than I could ever remember coming.

Having the three of them all touching me and rubbing me at the same time was almost too much. I shook as I came down from my orgasm, but I still found myself wanting more.

Julian pulled me on top of him and slid into me while I was still pulsing through my orgasm. Wrapping his arms around me, he kissed my throat, and I knew he was marking me, reminding me that he'd claimed me as his that first time, too.

Isaac rubbed my back and took my face in his hands to kiss me while Blake moved behind me. I gasped and tensed up when I felt Blake's fingers pushing into my ass.

"Don't tense up, baby. It's just like before. Did it feel good then?"

I moaned as I did as he said and nodded.

"Tell him, Red. Did him you liked when he fucked your ass."

"I liked when you fucked my ass, Blake."

"Good girl, Red."

Blake growled and added something cold to where his fingers were filling me. "Tell me if this is too much, baby."

I held my breath until Isaac pressed his lips to mine and then looked into my eyes.

"Breathe, Mal. We would never hurt you."

I kissed him harder as Blake pressed the head of his shaft against me and slowly pushed inside. I gasped into the kiss as the feeling of being too full took over. I dug my hands into Julian's chest and moaned.

Blake gripped my ass and inched himself into me until he was fully inside, his big cock stuffing me so full that I thought I would burst open. Squeezing my ass, he swore with a gravel voice. "Fucking hell, baby. You're taking me so beautifully. You were made for this, for us."

"We're going to fuck you now, Red." Julian pumped his hips into me in a fast thrust that almost made my eyes cross. "You feel like fucking heaven on me."

Isaac knelt beside us and fed me his cock even as Blake and Julian began moving. Blake pulled out first and then thrust back into me as Julian pulled out. They moved in sync, taking it easy on me until my moans grew louder and more desperate. I took Isaac deep as all three of them started moving faster, filling me with their big cocks.

I careened towards another orgasm fast and moaned around Isaac's cock so much that he swore and pulled out of me to regain his control. My loud cries filled the room until he pushed back into my mouth. It was all so much. Blake's hands on my ass were tight and almost punishing as he thrust into me faster and faster. Julian drove his cock into me over and over again, his hands on my shoulders, keeping me from moving.

My body tightened and tingled all over as I got even closer to falling apart. Isaac's hands tightened in my hair as he swore my name like a curse and sank more of his cock into my mouth.

Blake slapped my ass and then did it again, leaving it hot. "We're going to fill you, baby. Are you ready for all of us?"

My body couldn't handle more. Starting in my limbs, my orgasm crawled in until it reached my core and then shot out like a firework. A scream tore from my full mouth and my body went rigid. My core milked their cocks until Julian's thrust faltered and he swore.

Shaking, I came hard as Julian shot his seed deep in me. Isaac followed, feeding me his with his hands locked in my hair. Blake came last, his cock filling me as he came hard with a shout. All at once, I was full of their come, and my body kept shaking with pleasure. I felt like it would never end until Julian slipped out of my core and Blake pushed his fingers in and found that magic spot again. Thrusting his fingers into it again and again while still filling my ass, with Julian circling my clit, I came again with a scream unlike any I'd ever screamed. A flood of pleasure poured out of my body, rushing out around Blake's fingers.

I collapsed on top of Julian and cried out as pleasure ravaged my body. Finally, Blake gently pulled out of me and fell onto the bed beside us. Isaac collapsed on the other side and they each threw an arm over my back.

I didn't think I'd ever be able to move again. I didn't even know if I was alive. My body pulsed, suddenly empty and leaking a combination of our fluids. I felt wet all over and hot, but I couldn't even try to lift my head.

Julian held me tight. "Fuck."

Blake groaned. "Am I alive?"

Isaac grunted. "Not sure."

I moaned as another wave of pleasure washed over me. "I think I'm broken."

"I can assure you that you're fucking perfect." Blake stroked his hands over my ass and groaned again. "Jesus, you're perfect."

I shifted on top of Julian and felt the wetness again. "Did I pee?"

Julian chuckled. "No, Red. You did come like a fucking firehose, though."

"Oh, Isaac, I'm sorry."

"You're kidding, right?" He turned my face to his and grinned. "I'm going to hang these sheets on the wall as memorabilia. Don't you dare apologize."

I buried my face in Julian's chest and shivered. "How am I ever supposed to be able to have normal sex again?"

They all three growled in unison, making me laugh. Blake's grip on my ass tightened while Isaac's went to my hair again. His eyes were laser hot as he shook his head. "You're not supposed to. You have us."

I rolled my eyes and ignored him, afraid of letting myself think they were being serious.

"She rolled her eyes at you, didn't she?" Blake slapped my ass when Isaac nodded. "Your ass is sexy with my handprint on it. Do you want more?"

I wiggled, making Julian moan. "Don't you dare, Blake."

Julian was already hard again, head pressing against my entrance again. "Do it."

Exhausted, worn out, and wet, we ended up making love again, trading positions and coming with another mind-blowing orgasm. We passed out in a pile of sweaty bodies, unfed and unworried.

Still, I noticed when Julian slipped from the bed later and crept away into the night.

CHAPTER TWENTY

My hungry stomach sent me searching for food early the next morning. I left Isaac and Blake in bed and pulled on one of their t-shirts before raiding the kitchen. It didn't take long for me to settle on ice cream and grab a spoon to eat straight from the container. I was spoiling myself in other ways; I might as well eat what I really wanted, too, I figured.

I curled up on the couch and had just started eating when I heard footsteps behind me and turned to find both Isaac and Blake shuffling into the room. I smiled at their sleepy faces. They were ridiculously cute for two gruff-looking mountain men who liked doing really kinky shit in their free time.

Isaac sat on one side of me and pulled me against his bare chest while Blake sat on the other side and pulled my feet into his lap. They yawned in sync and looked me over.

Blake rubbed my legs and yawned again. "You're beautiful like this."

I ate another spoonful of ice cream and looked down at myself. "In a t-shirt?"

Isaac tugged at my hair. "In one of our shirts with your hair all messed up and makeup smeared all over your face."

I immediately rubbed at my face. "That's not a cute look."

"We think you're wrong." Blake shrugged and started massaging my feet. "Are you coming back to bed soon?"

I hid a smile with more ice cream. "Yeah. Missing me?"

Isaac grunted. "I don't want to sleep with this idiot if you're not there."

"Speak for yourself. Your mattress sucks. I would be in my own bed if not for Mal."

"There's nothing wrong with my mattress."

I grinned while listening to them bicker like little boys. "Did you always bicker like this?"

They looked at me like they hadn't even realized they were fighting. Blake frowned and shrugged. "I guess. Probably."

"Definitely. Especially Julian and Blake. They both think they're the boss."

I sighed. "Why'd he leave?"

Isaac went quiet for a minute, like he was waiting on Blake to explain, but when Blake didn't jump in, he finally spoke up. "There's a history here that has nothing to do with you. I mean, it's not your fault, and him leaving doesn't reflect on how he feels about you."

"What is it?"

Blake grabbed my ice cream and shoved a big bite into his mouth while gesturing for Isaac to go on.

Isaac swore. "You're a dick."

I rested my cold hand on Isaac's thigh. "Tell me."

He grabbed my hand and rubbed it to warm it before speaking. "Our last girlfriend. Grace. She did some damage."

I frowned, an ugly feeling of jealousy rearing its head. "What'd she do?"

Blake finally decided he could comment. "What didn't she do, honestly?"

"She nearly broke us apart. Julian hasn't been the same since. Not with us. He's just so angry all the time." Isaac sat up and rested his elbows on his knees. "She was fucking awful, and we didn't see it."

"She was jealous of how close we were. Despite the fact that we were serious about her. We cared for her and took care of her. She still couldn't handle our relationship to each other, though. It was sick."

I made a face. "She got involved with triplets. Did she think you three wouldn't be close?"

"She just decided she needed more and more. She started doing little things to push Julian out. We didn't know it was happening until it was almost too late. Julian had been alienated and didn't trust us anymore. While she was turning us against him, she was breaking him down. She wouldn't let him touch her."

Blake winced. "We weren't careful with him. She told us things about him, and we believed them, despite knowing better."

My chest ached for Julian, and I found myself wishing he would walk through the door so I could hold him. "That's so awful. Why'd she do that to him?"

"Money. At least that's what we assumed. Blake has the lumber company and I have the ranch. Julian never wanted anything for himself. He was happy to just work with us, doing whatever was needed. It seemed like Grace realized she couldn't get anything else from Julian, so she cut him out."

"What a fucking bitch." I took the ice cream back from Blake and ate another bite. "I mean, just a raging bitch. I can't believe she would do that to him."

Isaac combed his fingers through his hair and sighed. "Yeah. It was shocking that Julian even joined us last night. It shows how much he likes you."

"It also shows that we picked right this time. You're perfect for us."

My stomach sank as I thought of the secret I was holding back from all of them. I was hiding something huge from them. I was hiding Julian's son from him. I had been for a year. I had to believe that would hurt him.

It was something I'd never worried about before. I had only thought of myself and Hank. I'd never considered what not knowing about Hank might do to Julian. I put my hand over my mouth and winced, wondering what I was going to do.

"Mal?"

I looked up at Isaac and tried to clear away the panic from my face. "Yeah?"

"You okay?"

I nodded roughly. "Brain freeze."

There I went, lying again. They'd invited me into their home and business, trusted me with their secrets, trusted me with Julian, and there I was, lying. My stomach cramped as I thought about what I'd done and what I was going to do.

"Let's go back to bed." Isaac stretched and pulled me up. "You need more sleep."

I wasn't sure I'd ever sleep again. I'd seen the cracks in their relationship. I'd seen the way Julian seemed to exist on the outside and I felt like I was going to hurt them even more. I handed the ice cream to Blake when he reached for it and silently went back to the bed. Crawling into the middle, I was sandwiched by them and held while they fell asleep pretty much right away.

I'd known getting involved with them was a dangerous thing to do, but I hadn't figured on it hurting them. My worst nightmares had been about sharing custody with a man I didn't know at all. I'd been worried about losing Hank, even partially.

It was too late to change anything, but that didn't stop me from feeling like a piece of shit. I was so selfish.

I was also terrified about what happened next. I couldn't keep things a secret forever. I liked the guys. I even liked Julian's rough personality. I liked being with them and feeling like I fit with them. Their comments about me being perfect for them had slipped through the cracks in my armor and built little shrines of a future. I was thinking about dating, something I hadn't allowed myself to do in too long.

None of my feelings mattered, though, because I'd hidden something so huge from them. They were going to hate me. They were going to think I was a liar, like Grace.

And who the hell was Grace? Was she still in town? Could I find her and punch her in the boob for hurting them? Maybe I needed to punch myself in the boob.

I shifted between my two burly men, men who I had no right to really claim. I wanted them. I wanted Julian. It might not matter, though. Not after they found out about Hank.

"Whatever it is, we'll sort through it, Mal." Isaac's calm voice was a soothing balm that I didn't feel like I deserved.

Still, I turned my face into his chest and squeezed my eyes shut to hold the tears in. I didn't know how he was reading me. I thought he was sleeping, but he was still there, trying to take care of me.

"It's okay, baby. Cry if you need to." Blake wrapped his arm around my stomach and kissed my shoulder. "We're here."

"Why?" My voice broke as I said it, and the tears came hard and fast.

Isaac stroked my hair. "If you haven't noticed, we like you."

"You fit with us. You're funny and smart." Blake stroked my stomach with his big hand. "And you're absolutely beautiful."

"We just know. It's not typical for all three of us to like the same person. We're different men with different needs, but you shine to all of us." Isaac wiped my tears and sighed. "Even Julian. Seeing him talk to you is like watching some of his old self come out."

"We haven't spent a lot of time with you, but we know what we know. Call it a triplet thing." Blake combed his fingers through my hair. "And whatever you're so worried about won't be too big for us to sort through."

I choked my feelings out through my tears. "I just don't deserve this. I'm horrible."

"You're not." Isaac growled. "Now, stop it. You're running on too little sleep and coming off of a pretty big experience. You need rest."

I sniffled and suddenly felt just how tired I really was. I yawned and curled into them. My brain slowed with the steady stroking of my hair from Blake. My eyes were so heavy that I let them close and sighed. "I hope you don't hate me."

Isaac shh-ed me and kissed my forehead. "We couldn't hate you. Now go to sleep."

CHAPTER TWENTY-ONE

Kara came and got me from work the next day, her excuse that she missed Hank and me, but I knew her true motives. She wanted gossip. Lucky for her, I was feeling like spilling my guts. I told her to pick me up with lunch already in the car if she wanted me. There was no way I was going out in public until I absolutely had to. Not when everyone knew I was boning the Steele brothers.

She didn't disappoint, which was how I knew she was desperate for the tea. She showed up with an entire pizza and two massive slices of chocolate cake, to be paired expertly with a giant Diet Coke. I strapped Hank into his car seat and then sank into the passenger seat.

"You look...rough." Kara looked me over, the smile dying on her lips instantly. "What happened, Mal?"

I calmly put on my seatbelt and stared straight ahead. "Just drive, okay?"

"Jesus. Did you rob the place? What's with the grim expression?" Even while questioning me, she pulled out of the lot and drove away from town. "There's an overlook up here that we can park at."

"Julian is Hank's father!" I screeched the words out and then buried my face in my hands. "Oh, god. I said it. I said it and it's out there."

Kara slammed the car to a stop on the side of the road. "What?"

I looked back to check on Hank and then turned to face her. "Hank. Julian Steele is his father."

"No, that's impossible. You just started dating him."

"I'm not dating." I shook my head. "I mean, no, never mind. I slept with him before. It was that day I met you at the bar after I left that asshole Niall."

"I'm not understanding."

I tugged at my hair. "I had sex with Julian that day. In the parking lot. We slept together and I got carried away and didn't use protection. Hence, the little bundle of joy in the backseat."

"You're shitting me."

"I wish I was, Kara. I really wish I was." I dry heaved, the stress turning my stomach. "I'm going to throw up."

Kara pushed me away from her while rolling down the window. "Not in my car! I just got it cleaned!"

I laughed through a dry heave, hysterical. "Are you kidding? That's not supportive."

"Sorry that I'm not being supportive when you're telling me that you had Julian Steele's baby! I'm having a little bit of a hard time computing this. You sleep with Julian and get pregnant, and then what? Did you tell him? Did he know this whole time?" She looked at my face and then swore. "You never told him. He still doesn't know, does he?"

"No. None of them know. I'm a monster."

"How the fuck did I manage to set you up with a set of triplets, one of whom fathered your fucking child?" She rubbed the bridge of her nose. "Obviously, you need to tell them. Julian deserves to know he has a son. And as much as Julian isn't my favorite Steele brother, he'll be a good father."

I shoved open the car door and hung my head out the side to get some fresh air. "Everything's going to change."

"Yeah, it is. Hank will have a father. And uncles. He'll have a bigger family and more love." She smacked my arm. "And you'll be fine. This doesn't mean you're losing Hank. He's your baby, Mallory. No one can take him from you. You're a good mother."

I blinked away tears. "I don't know how any of this happened, honestly. I thought I could stay away from this place, away from Julian. I didn't even know his last name. I thought he'd never know or care. And then you set me up with his identical triplet, and it all went to shit. I like them. I like them a lot and I'm going to blow it all up."

"Side note. I did really fucking great setting you up, didn't I? I knew you'd be just kinky enough to love having three men. And they're good men. Good men who are a good match for you. They like you. They're not going to drop you. Just explain things to them."

"I think I might just throw up instead."

"Not in the car."

"I know!"

"You don't have to shout at me. I'm sitting right here." She sniffed like she was upset. "It's not like I'm the one who got you knocked up with a Steele baby."

"Kara, I'll push you off the overlook and be glad for it."

She laughed. "Relax, Mal. Yeah, this is big, but the guys will understand. You're just going to have to talk to them. Today. Now. Literally right now. I'll drive you back."

"No! I can't just tell them right now. I'm not ready."

"Too bad. You have to talk to them. The longer you wait, the worse it'll be." She didn't even wait on me to close to car door before she pulled back on the road and headed towards Steele Lumber. "I can't believe you got knocked up by Julian Steele."

I shouted at her as I slammed the car door shut. "Are you trying to kill me?"

"And leave me with the responsibility of telling Julian? Yeah, right."

"You're making this worse!"

"That's impossible." She looked over at me and sighed. "I mean, it's fine. Things are fine."

"I'm so glad you're taking me back. I can't wait to get out of this car and get away from you. I'm so mad at you! You were the least helpful you've ever been!"

Kara laughed, and it eventually got me, too. When we were both laughing, she pulled over again and turned off the car. "I thought you were a bratty teenager again for a second there."

I wiped my eyes, suddenly crying. "I just feel like I made so many mistakes. And then I came here to start something different. I don't even know what I wanted, but just something better than being alone in the city. Now I've made a mess of this. What am I supposed to do?"

"You haven't made a mess, Mal. You'll sort it out with the guys and things will be okay. Better than okay because you already have a family with them. They just don't know it yet."

"Everyone knows I'm sleeping with three guys at the same time. Did you really know that was going to happen when you set me up with Isaac?"

Stroking my cheek and pushing my hair back out of my face, Kara smiled. "I had an idea. Everyone does know that the brothers prefer to act as one. They also know that they haven't had anyone special in their lives since that twat Grace. I guess I thought they'd be good for you. A man for every occasion. And god, I have to believe the sex is everything. Not that you'll tell me anything about it."

"I can't go out in public. Do you know how it feels to know that everyone knows I'm having wild sex with three brothers at once?" I cringed. "I have three holes, Kara. There are three brothers. You do the math!"

She'd just taken a drink of her coke and spewed it all over the windshield of the car. With a screaming laugh, she looked over at me and then down at my crotch. "Oh, my god!"

I groaned. "Kara! That's what I'm afraid everyone is going to do!"

"No. No! They won't." She giggled. "They won't!"

"It doesn't even matter. The guys aren't going to want to touch me after I tell them about Hank. I'm going to be known as that twat Mallory around town. Which is somehow a demotion from Mallory who takes it up the ass."

Kara was crying then, laughing so hard that she was squeezing her legs together and grabbing at my arm. "Stop! I'm going to pee on myself!"

Hank started screaming along in the backseat, his happy screams just as ear-piercing as his angry screams. I sighed, defeated. "You can pee at the office if you head back that way."

"Fine, fine." She started the car and drove back to the office, still laughing as she did. "Go in there and tell them now. I'll be there, so if things go poorly, I'll get you out. Not that I think they will."

I waved her away. "Just go pee. I'll figure this out myself."

She hurried inside, leaving me to get Hank and my food from the car. I'd just eat inside without Kara. My food would probably taste better if I wasn't being laughed at while I ate it.

I walked in and dropped my food off before walking over to peek into Blake's office to see if he was in. He was at his desk, looking at his computer, when he spotted me. I smiled and waved. "Just seeing if you were in."

"Come here, baby." He pushed away from the desk and patted his lap.

I chewed on my top lip and moved closer to him. "You call me that like you've known me forever."

He smiled and pulled me down, gently since I was still holding Hank. "Wishful thinking, maybe."

I felt myself blush and turned so I could wrap my arm around him and press my face into his neck. I really hoped that he would be able to get past what I had to tell him. Hank yanked at my hair, and I found myself even sadder when Blake gently pulled my hair out of Hank's fingers.

"Everything's going to be okay, Mal."

"See, Mal! I told you he wasn't going to freak out." Kara strolled into his office and grinned at us. "Why wouldn't he be excited about finding out Hank is Julian's—"

"Kara!" I shot out of Blake's lap and stood next to his desk, rigid. I'd startled Hank, and he started a slow cry that grew bigger the longer I didn't soothe him. I couldn't, though. I was too busy panicking about how Kara had just dropped the bomb on Blake for me.

"What did you say?" Blake's voice was too calm, too low. He sounded angry.

Kara stammered. "Um. I thought you'd already told him, Mallory. That's why I came in and did the thing when I heard him comforting you. Why didn't you tell him? Oh, god."

"Just a fucking second." Blake held up his hands and looked at me. "Did she really just say that Hank, that Hank, the one you're holding, is Julian's? Julian, as in my brother? As in you had my brother's baby?"

"Don't swear at my sister, Blake Steele. I'll rip your balls off and mount them to my dashboard." Kara came out blazing, teeth bared and eyes furious.

Blake actually winced. "I'm not swearing at her. I think I was swearing at you."

"Oh, then, that's fine." Back to normal, Kara shrugged and looked at me. "I'm so sorry, Mal. I didn't mean to do that."

"Before I swear at anyone again, someone had better answer my question."

I finally clicked back into action and rocked Hank against my chest. Turning to face Blake, I blinked back tears and nodded. "He's Julian's."

Sinking into his chair, Blake scrubbed his hands over his face and then stood back up. "Okay. I wasn't expecting that."

"I know. I'm so sorry I kept it from you. I just... I was scared." I groaned when I realized I was already crying. "It's not a good excuse for what I did, but I am sorry."

"Does Julian know?"

I shook my head. "Not yet."

Groaning, Blake walked over to me and pulled me into a hug. "You need to tell him."

I nodded against his chest and held onto his warmth and comfort for as long as I could before he backed away and looked down at Hank. "I'm going to tell him. I'm just...I'm still scared. I don't want to upset him. I know I'm no better than Grace, though, and what she did to him. Maybe I'm even worse."

Kara snorted. "No fucking way you're anywhere near that. You're a good and decent woman and if Blake here doesn't see that and tell you that soon, I'll have to remind him of the balls on the dash thing."

Blake growled. "Relax, big sis; I know that she's amazing. I'm crazy about her."

I handed Hank to Kara and walked away. "I just need a second."

Retreating to the bathroom, I didn't even get the door shut before Blake was there, pushing me farther into the room and closing the door behind him. We were in the dark, but then he wrapped his arms around me and tugged me into his chest.

The nearly two years of keeping things together and trying to be everything I could be were catching up to me. I had this consuming fear that it was all coming crashing down on me and that I was going to lose everything in the end. Like somehow even Hank would be taken away and I'd be left completely alone.

"Shh, baby, you're fine." Blake stroked my hair and kissed the top of my head. "You're freaking out a little, aren't you? But things are okay. The secret's out and things are going to be okay."

"You keep saying things are okay. Are they not okay? Julian is going to freak out, isn't he? He's going to be hurt that I kept it a secret. I took a year of Hank's life from him. He'll hate me. If he hates me, you can't be with me. You have to pick him."

"You're getting ahead of yourself." Feeling around until he found the light and flicked it off, he held my face in his hands and tipped my face up to his. "We'll tell him together. He'll probably be cranky, but that's nothing new. He'll get over it, especially when he gets over it and realizes he has a son."

My stomach fluttered. "I didn't know any of this was going to happen. I just feel so scared."

"Of what, Mal?"

"Of losing everything." I looked down at my feet. "Of losing Hank."

"No one is going to take Hank from you. They'd have to go through me first. Do you understand me? Now, come on. We need to go talk to Julian."

CHAPTER TWENTY-TWO

Kara insisted on keeping Hank when I left with Blake. She also didn't let me leave until she'd threatened Blake within an inch of his life. She'd gone full-on momma bear, and I loved her all the more for it, even if I was the one who'd done the hurting.

On the way to Isaac's, Blake held my hand and mentioned a time or two how scary Kara was. He drove slowly towards the ranch, giving me time to get myself together. I didn't know if any amount of time was going to help. My hands were shaking and I felt like I was going to throw up. I felt it in my gut that Julian wasn't going to react the way I hoped he would. He was going to be angry, rightfully so. That didn't make it any less hard to walk into. Even if I deserved him hating me, I didn't want him to.

"He's got big emotions. He always has. He's quicker to react, but he loves hard and gives everything when he decides to. That shit with Grace fucked with him, and he's been more reclusive than ever, but the old Julian is still there."

"I hope I didn't just break the old Julian."

"Just keep breathing." Blake turned off towards the ranch and squeezed my hand. "I'll be there for you."

I realized I was holding my breath and forced myself to blow the air out and suck in another breath. I hated confrontation. As sassy as I could be, I never wanted people to dislike me. I didn't want to be the bad guy. There was just no getting around it, though.

Isaac and Julian were sitting on the porch when Blake parked his truck. They both stood up and moved towards us, but I couldn't get out.

Blake undid my seatbelt and cupped the back of my neck. "Just be honest."

"If only I'd taken that advice a while ago."

"Come on." He climbed out and went to move around to open my door, but Julian moved in.

Opening my door and stepping in, Julian cupped my chin and turned my face to his. "What's going on, Red?"

I squeezed my eyes shut, the epitome of maturity. "Oh, Julian."

Isaac swore in the background and drew Julian's attention. Seeing his brothers staring at him, Julian stiffened. "What is it, Red?"

I forced myself to look up at him and meet his cautious gaze. "I...I have something I need to tell you."

"I got that part, Mallory. What is it?" He'd already started shutting down. I could feel it in his body.

I winced at hearing him say my full name. "I'm so sorry. I just didn't know how to tell you before. I was stupid and scared. I just—"

"Just spit it the fuck out."

I glanced up and saw Blake moving towards us, his brows furrowed. I knew that I was messing things up for them. Looking back at Julian, I dug my fingernails into my thighs. "I got pregnant after we had sex. The first time."

He frowned and shook his head. "What?"

"I got pregnant. And I had the baby. Hank. I had Hank. He's yours." I swallowed and tried to rush on to get everything out. "I know that I should've told you as soon as I found out; I should've come back here and found you. I should've told you as soon as I got back here and met Isaac. I did so many things wrong. I'm so sorry. I'm so sorry I didn't tell you sooner."

He stumbled back a step, and then anger burned to life in his eyes. "They knew?"

I blinked, stunned stupid by the question. "What?"

Jerking his head towards his brothers, he growled. "They knew, didn't they? They knew, and they didn't tell me."

I watched in horror as Julian stormed towards his brothers, fury clear on his face. "No, Julian! They didn't know!"

It was too late. Julian spotted the frustration on Blake's face and centered his ire on him. "What was it this time? Did you think it'd be easier to edge me out if I didn't know she had my fucking kid?"

Blake tried to deny the accusations, but Julian caught him off guard with a punch to the chin. Blake stumbled back a step and then came back even harder at Julian. Isaac did his best to push them apart but then Julian swung at him, too.

"Stop!" I ran towards them screaming, my heart in my throat. I'd never seen grown men fight, and I didn't ever want to see it again, especially men I cared about. "Stop it!"

"You fuckers are always pushing me out! You did this, didn't you?" Julian was raging, a cut on his lip bleeding. "That's my kid! You were going to take him, too?"

Isaac grabbed Julian in a headlock and tried to hold him steady, but then Blake landed a hard punch to Julian's stomach that just kept the fight going. "We just found out, asshole! Stop fucking fighting us. You're going to get yourself hurt!"

I grabbed Blake and tried to pull him, but he was too strong. He just dragged me closer to the fight. "It's my fault! Be mad at me! Please, stop!"

Blake threw another punch at Julian, but Julian managed to turn Isaac into it. Julian lashed out at Blake, but Blake swung his big body backward to dodge it and elbowed me in the face.

I went down hard, my mouth instantly throbbing while little birds circled over my head. I blinked as my vision straightened and I looked up to find the three brothers being separated by ranch hands who'd seen the fight and come running. I rubbed my jaw and felt blood dripping from my split lip, but I wasn't too bad off, from what I could tell. The hit had definitely knocked some of the panic out of me, though.

Isaac was the first one to notice that I was on the ground, bleeding. He swore and shook off the man holding him to come to my side. "Shit, Mal. You okay?"

Blake and Julian realized what'd happened next, and Blake's face paled. "Oh, fuck, baby. I did that, didn't I? I'm so fucking sorry. Oh, fuck."

Julian stood still, his arms still being held by two men. He looked me over and then at his brothers kneeling on each side of me. There was pain clear in his eyes, but it hardened to anger as I watched. "Cute family."

I pulled myself to my feet and winced when my entire face ached. "Julian, this is all my fault. They didn't know. I was trying to figure out how to tell you. I didn't mean to do this. I don't want to do this. I don't want you to fight."

"Too bad." Julian shook himself free and turned away. "You know what? You three can do whatever the fuck you want, but I'm not doing this again. I'm not doing this shit."

"And what if I want you? What if I want you here with us?" My voice broke, and I took a deep breath. "I was wrong not to tell you about Hank. He deserves you in his life."

Julian stopped, but he didn't turn to look back at me. "You don't even know me. Just tell him Blake or Isaac is his dad and he'll never have to know."

"Goddammit, Julian, I want you here!" I walked after him, my heart pounding. I realized I was pouring out my stupid heart in front of a bunch of random men, but I was desperate. "I've thought of you almost every day since that first time. I wondered what things could've been like if they were different. I should've found you and told you, but I was just so fucking scared."

Spinning around and glaring at me, Julian pointed at me and then dropped his hand. "Just stop it. You made the decision to keep me out of your life and Hank's life every day since he was born. If you think you need me to have my brothers, you don't. They don't have a ton of loyalty to the fuck-up brother."

"Just listen to me!"

"Fuck that. I'm done here." He looked me over and shook his head. "I'm going back to my cabin. I don't need any of this bullshit."

I watched as he stomped off to his motorcycle and roared away on it. I stood there, feeling like I'd ruined everything. My face hurt, and I'd just put the final nail in the coffin that was the Steele brothers' relationship. I didn't even want to face them.

"Can someone give me a ride home?" I kept my eyes on the ground and wrapped my arms around myself.

"Come inside and talk to us, Mal. Let me put some ice on your...face. Jesus." Isaac appeared in front of me and frowned when he looked at me. "We definitely need to get some ice on that."

"I want to go home. I think I need Kara."

Blake's face was grim as he stood in front of me and looked me over. "I'll take you. I deserve whatever murder attempt she'll have for me."

"Mal, you didn't do this. This was a long time coming." Isaac sighed and gently kissed my forehead. "This isn't over."

I just nodded and walked back to Blake's truck. I got in and buckled my seatbelt, eyes straight ahead as Blake got in and started the truck. My heart was in my throat. I felt like I'd just ruined their relationship and ruined whatever chance Hank had with his father. All because I'd been selfish and cruel. I was a monster.

"I am so fucking sorry, Mal. I can't believe I hurt you." Blake's voice shook with emotion. "I swear to you that I didn't mean to do that."

I choked back a sob and looked at him. "I don't care about my face. I know you didn't mean to. You need to be more worried about what just happened with Julian. I broke your relationship."

"Fuck that. That fight has been in the making for years. We'll be fine." Shaking his head, he reached over and grabbed my hand. "And I care about your face. I care that I hurt you."

"It's only fair after I hurt you."

"Fuck, Mallory, you didn't hurt me. You might've hurt Julian, but you didn't mean to. And he'll get over it. You can't be this hard on yourself."

I pulled my hand away from him and turned into my window. "I hate myself right now. I don't want to hear you try to make me feel better. I don't deserve it."

"Dammit, Mallory, this isn't productive."

We were just outside of Kara's neighborhood, so I managed to hold my tongue until we were in her driveway. Then, I just threw open the door and jumped out, hurrying up to the front door. I let myself in and hurried up to my room, stopping only after I closed and locked my bedroom door. Leaning against it, I let myself cry finally.

Barely a few seconds passed before Kara was at my door and knocking to come in. When I didn't act fast enough, she unlocked the door somehow and slipped in. Taking one look at my face, she swore and moved to leave, but I caught her arm.

"I tried to break up a fight. No one tried to do this."

She shook with anger. "I'm still going to murder them. All three of them. Unless there were other people involved, too. Maybe I'll just murder the entire fucking town. You need ice and pain meds."

I sank onto my bed and blinked through tears. "I just need to have you hold me while I cry like you used to."

"Oh, honey." Sitting next to me, she wrapped me in her arms and held me tight. "It's all going to be okay. I promise."

Full out sobbing, I wasn't sure how it would be. Okay felt impossible.

CHAPTER TWENTY-THREE

Because I was still feeling like a child, I let Kara call out of work for me the next few days. There was no way I wanted to face Blake or Isaac before I was prepared for it, but I also couldn't chance people seeing my face and assuming the worst. My mouth stayed swollen for the rest of the week, and a nasty bruise had marred the bottom half of my face, radiating out from my lips. My eyes were also swollen from all the crying I'd done. I looked and felt like a wreck.

Kara had been running interference for me, as well as everything else she was doing. She'd even taken a day off of work to stay home and hang out with me. Every time Isaac or Blake tried to reach me, she'd been blocking them, though. I just wasn't ready to face them and she knew it. She'd threatened them plenty, but they still kept coming back. Blake had even brought flowers and an edible arrangement that both said he was sorry.

I didn't know what to say to them. They needed to choose Julian. They loved their brother, and he needed to see that. As much as I didn't want to find myself without them, I wanted them to be okay even more. I wanted Julian to come back to them and for them to heal. I'd messed their relationship up even more than Grace had. They all just needed to forget about me.

As I held Hank, I knew they couldn't, though. I'd managed to intwine myself in their lives permanently. That just made me feel even worse about myself. Julian would never be free of me. Not really.

I wasn't sure what came next. I knew that I couldn't hide forever, though, so when Kara started making demands that I go to the grocery store with her, I gave in without too much of a fight. It was the middle of the day on a Saturday, and I figured I wouldn't run into the triplets there.

I applied a lot of makeup to hide the state of my face and got Hank ready before letting Kara lead me out to her car. I buckled Hank in and sat in the front quietly while Kara drove.

Finally, she gave in to the need to check in on me. "How are you feeling today?"

I grunted. "I'm fine."

"Uh-huh. You look fine."

I glared at her for a second before pulling down the visor and checking out my makeup in the small mirror. "It's fine. The make-up's a little thick, but it's not anything that is going to scare small children."

She laughed. "I just meant your overall look. Your face looks fine. It's your mental state that I'm more worried about."

I watched the town go by out of my window and sighed. "I don't know, Kara. I just... I'm sad. It didn't take very long for them to crawl under my skin."

"Obviously, you got under theirs, too. They've been calling non-stop." She took my hand and held it. "I think you should call them back and try to work this out."

"Did you ever think you would be trying to help me work out issues in a fucking reverse harem? Like, actively encouraging me to try my hardest to keep fucking three men at the same time?"

"You're going to have to learn to watch your mouth in front of Hank soon. Or his first real word is going to be fucking."

That brought a smile to my lips. "Like mine was, you mean?"

"Yeah. It wasn't as cute as your smile suggests you think it was. Mom and Dad got in an awful fight over it. They each blamed each other and then me, somehow." Kara shook her head. "I know that you're panicking and thinking the worst about yourself, Mal. You've always done that. You cut yourself down so hard and fast. You've seen what bad parents and bad partners look like. You're not going to make those same mistakes with Hank."

I sighed and made the effort of putting my hair into a bun while I thought of what I wanted to say. "I feel like I've already made so many mistakes."

"He's a happy, healthy baby. He's on track developmentally, and so far, he's never even had a scratch. I'd say you're doing pretty well. I'd dropped Taylor once by the time he was one."

"I remember. Tyler just about had a stroke."

"Yeah. So, you're doing fine."

"How can you say that after what I did with Julian?"

Kara parked in front of the grocery store on Main Street and turned to face me. "Because it's all going to be fine in the end. I have a feeling."

I pulled Hank out of the car and looked at my sister over the roof of her car. "I'm glad one of us feels any kind of positive."

She grabbed a buggy someone had left in front of the store and brought it over to me so I could put Hank in it. "One of us is able to see more than her imagined failures."

I focused on settling Hank in the buggy, and then we were in the store and our conversation went to being focused on what we were buying. Kara loaded up the cart like a madwoman while I meandered and added sweets when I saw them. I'd cleared the house out of everything fattening by way of my mouth. I was a stress eater. And a happy eater. And just an eater. I couldn't help it.

Kara was mid-toss, throwing a bottle of ketchup into the cart, when her eyes went wide and her face scrunched up in the way that it did when she saw something she didn't like. She immediately grabbed the front of the cart and started tugging me along. "Let's go get stuff for salad."

"Ugh, Kara. I don't want salad. You've made me eat salad at least once a day. You're going to give me a complex."

"I'm only making you eat salads because the only other thing you're eating is candy. Or cookies. Or all of the leftover valentine's chocolates that Tyler got me."

"Those were over a month old, Kara. I did you a favor." I was practically racing to keep up with her, she was moving so fast. "Slow down, woman. This isn't a sprint."

"Oh, fuck." Kara all but shouted the words as she rounded the corner of an aisle and nearly ran over a pretty blond woman. Glancing back at me, I saw her eyes go all wonky, like she was trying to tell me something.

I didn't speak Kara's eyes, though, so I just waited on her to go around the blond. When the blond didn't move, either, I looked up and saw she was looking at me with a critical eye. I raised my eyebrows and looked at Kara.

"Grace, it's been a while." Kara finally acknowledged the woman and put a barely there smile on her face. It almost looked more like she was smelling something terrible.

My stomach tightened at hearing the name. Surely the pretty little blond in front of us wasn't the same Grace that had hurt Julian. Yet, I knew instantly that it was, judging by the way she was trying to scalp me with her eyes.

"Kara. And is this the famous Mallory I've heard so much about?" Her mouth pinched and turned down as she looked me over. "The stories really do flatter you."

I tilted my head to the side and stared at her. Surely, she wasn't trying to be a mean girl to me. I didn't even know her. "I'm Mallory. I don't believe I know you. Are you a friend of Kara's?"

Kara gave me a thumbs-up behind her back and smiled a real smile. "We just see each other around sometimes."

"I find it hard to believe that you haven't heard mention of me around. After all, we dated the same men." Grace adjusted her purse on her arm and looked me over again, her gaze settling on my hips. "It's just crazy how taste can change from one year to the next."

I cleared my throat to cut Kara off from whatever she was about to lash out at the mean woman with. "Seems like it. Can we help you with something? We're just picking up a few things and then heading back home."

"That's right; I heard that things aren't going well with you and the Steele brothers."

I bit my lip and shook my head. I was going to remain nice if it was the last thing I ever did. No way was I getting into some kind of boob measuring contest with her. "Rumors sure do travel fast in such a small town."

"You shouldn't give in to such gossip, Grace. It's not a good look." Kara pushed the cart away from Grace and sent a teeth-bared smile her way. "We've got shopping to do, if you don't mind."

Grace reached out and put her hand on the buggy, stopping it. "Is that really Julian's kid?"

"Whatever you're about to do, rethink it." Kara was bristling up, ready to fight.

"I was just thinking about how pathetic it is to have a kid with the poor one. And you still couldn't keep them. Honestly, I'm shocked. I know that if I would've given in to their desires for kids, they never would've let me go when I left. Not that they don't still send me those lost puppy looks all the time."

"The poor one?" I laughed, my anger rearing its ugly head. "Lady, I don't know you or what you're all about, but it's abundantly clear that you have about as much heart as a brick wall. It's obvious that you still don't fully understand what you lost when you let them get away. Or maybe you do and that's why you're here, bothering me like a yippy little dog. Either way, I want nothing to do with it. I'm stressed, I'm tired, and I'm a mom now, so I'm not going to scream at you in a grocery store."

Kara leaned into her. "Fuck with my baby sister and I'll end you. I know where the skeletons in your closet hang out, Grace."

"You're never going to be enough for them." Needing one last dig, she looked at our buggy and laughed. "Or maybe the problem is that you're more than enough. Too much, even."

Kara reached for her, but I managed to grab her arm just before she made contact. Thankfully, Grace was already turning and didn't see her life flash before her eyes. "I'll kill her. I'll club her to death with a jar of pickles and hide her in the canned meat, where they put the rest of the fake shit."

I blew out a breath and shook my head. "She's awful."

"Worse than awful." Kara turned back to me and grunted. "You should've let me grab her. It would've been worth jail time."

"Did the guys really like her? I mean, she's pretty, but she's literally so mean."

"She had them fooled." Rubbing her eyes, Kara looked at the stuff in our buggy and nodded. "We need more chocolate."

I stared after Grace and frowned. "I mean, she's really, really mean. I'm not like that."

"Duh."

"I mean, I'm not like her."

Kara blinked. "I know. You're great, and she's a flying twatwaffle."

"I'm nothing like her. I don't feel any of those awful things about Julian. I like Julian." I shook my head and tried to process everything I was feeling. "Shit. I'm not like her!"

"What the fuck is happening to you?"

"I want good things for the guys. I want them to come together again. I want Julian to feel like part of his family. I'm not a sabotaging monster like that woman. I thought I was just as bad as her, and that I was unforgiveable, but after talking to her, I know that I couldn't do as much damage as she did. I don't think anyone could. She's a demon."

Kara threw her hands up. "That's what I've been saying."

"I think I threw in the towel too fast."

"Yeah! You think?"

"I can make it right. Even if Julian doesn't want me, I can try to fix their relationship. And I can help Julian have a son." I scooped Hank out of the buggy and smiled at Kara. "I love you. Thanks for always being willing to fight for me."

"You know I love you, too. Now, go get your men." She looked at Hank and made a face. "Maybe leave him with me?"

"No, Julian is going to have to make the decision to walk away from Hank while looking at Hank if he tries to do that again." I backed away. "Do you happen to know where Julian's cabin is?"

"I do."

"Well?"

"Sorry. I can't seem to remember the directions. You're going to have to ask Blake or Isaac."

"You're an asshole."

"If I'm an asshole, you're an asshole."

"I'm leaving now."

"Or you could help me finish the shopping and I could give you a ride home."

I frowned. "I forgot that I didn't drive myself here."

She laughed while I put Hank back in the buggy and tapped my foot. "She has a lightning bolt of reality strike her ass and now she's in a big rush."

"Come on, lady. Let's get what we need and get out of here. I'm sure there are other exes lurking around the corners, and I just want to get out of here and get started on fixing things." I shivered. "Plus, I forgot about these people knowing about the butt stuff."

Throwing her head back in a ridiculously loud laugh, Kara drew nearly every eye in the place to us. Wiping tears from her eyes, she pointed me towards the deli. "Speaking of butt. We're having BBQ tomorrow. Get it? A Boston butt?"

I sighed. "This is my punishment for hurting Julian, isn't it?"

CHAPTER TWENTY-FOUR

I felt like I had a better chance at convincing Isaac to give me directions than I did with Blake. Blake was bossier out of the two of them, and I had a feeling he'd try to drive me to Julian's. I didn't want that, though. I needed to talk to Julian alone and show him that I was making an effort just for him. If I had any chance of fixing things, that would be the only way. I needed to show him that I cared about him as an individual.

By the time I got back to my car and drove to Isaac's, it was late afternoon. I wasn't sure where he'd be, but as soon as I pulled into the driveway, he came stalking out of the barn.

Seeing him made my chest ache, and I had to remind myself that I wasn't there to reconcile. Not yet. Not until I knew where things were with Julian. I stood just outside of my car and waited for him to close the gap between us. Watching him move towards me was hard. In just the few short days since I'd seen him, I'd almost managed to convince myself the magnetism that radiated from him was in my head.

"Mal. Are you okay?"

I smiled shyly and nodded. "What does it say about my exit that that's the first thing you ask me?"

"We've been worried." He shoved his hands in his pockets and looked over my face. "You look better."

I laughed. "Liar."

"Tell me you're here to come back to us." Sighing, Isaac suddenly looked older than his years. He ran his hands through his hair and tugged at it. "I fucking miss seeing you around here."

I bit my lip hard. I wanted to go to him and make us both feel better. "I have to make things right with Julian first."

Blowing out a big breath, Isaac nodded. "Okay."

"You know why, right?" I gripped the door frame that separated us hard. "I mean, you know that I care about you. I want this. I just... I can't do it if the three of you aren't okay."

"It fucking figures that the woman we fall for cares enough about the three of us that it's all or nothing." Shaking his head, he grabbed my arm and pulled me into his chest. "I get it. I'm just not loving it."

"I'm going to see Julian. He deserves an apology and a chance to see that I don't want him just because he's connected to you and Blake." I hugged him back and breathed in his warm scent. "Can you give me his address?"

"I'll take you."

"No. I need to do it alone." I pulled away and looked up at him. "I need to show him how I feel without you or Blake there."

"Dammit, Mal, you don't have to do it alone. The road isn't the best up around the cabin. And there are sometimes unsavory characters that hang around up there."

I raised my brows. "Unsavory characters?"

"That's for Julian to talk to you about, but I don't think you should go alone."

"Okay. I don't know what that means, but I don't care. I'm going." I got back in the car and rolled the window down. "You tell me or I'm going to Blake. One of you has to give in eventually. I have to do this. I feel sick to my stomach thinking I hurt him and thinking that I hurt your relationship. This is important to me."

"It's not your responsibility to fix us, Mal."

"Okay, I'll go see Blake."

Staring at me for a few seconds, Isaac finally swore and grabbed my phone through the open window. "I'm typing in the address into your GPS, but it won't matter once you get up the mountain. I'll tell you how to get there. You need to go straight there so you're not driving in the dark. Have Julian drive you back down. Don't put yourself at risk."

"I'll be safe."

"Drive even slower than you think you need to drive." He handed my phone back to me and rubbed his forehead. "Don't make me regret giving you that."

"You're cute when you worry."

"I'm serious, Mal."

"I am, too."

Opening the door, he leaned in and kissed me. It was slightly too hard for my sore lips, but my body instantly responded to him. I grabbed his hair and tugged him away. "I have to make things right first."

"No matter what happens with Julian, you're still mine, Mal." He stroked his thumb over the pulse in my throat and growled. "You're infuriating. Call me if you need anything. I'll come drive you home if you need me to."

I nodded. "Yes, sir."

"Blake's the one big on that boss shit, but I'm starting to see why." Kissing me again, he leaned back and quickly went over the directions for how to get to the cabin. "Don't make me regret this."

I smiled. "It's not like you really had a choice."

"Go. Before I show you what choice I have."

I hesitated and looked him over. "Just in case this doesn't go well."

"Goddammit, Mal. Even if Julian fucks up today, it's not forever. I'm not giving up." He backed away and shook his head. "Neither is Blake. You can only hide from us and ignore us for so long. Kara won't always be there to scare Blake away."

I bit my lip to hide a smile. I didn't mean to encourage him in case things did go poorly with Julian. "Oh, I saw Grace today. She's great."

Isaac actually blushed. His lips pursed, and he crossed his arms over his chest and kicked at the dirt like a little boy. "Not our best choice. I can see and admit that now."

"She's a big fan of mine, though." Smiling, I waved and started backing away. "Big, big fan."

I passed Blake while leaving the ranch and I was afraid he was going to stop and follow me, but Isaac must've stopped him. It was important that I go alone. Alone with Hank. I needed Julian to listen to me without his anger at his brothers getting in the way.

The drive to the base of the mountain was nice and peaceful, but within ten minutes of driving up the mountain, the road grew treacherous and car sickness hit me hard. On one side of the road was a wall of rock, on the other a sharp drop-off that seemed to just go on forever. The farther up I went, the narrower the road got. I passed several different turn-offs and kept going until there felt like nothing left. The trees were thicker; the sun was blocked out. It was almost eerie in the wake of Isaac's warnings.

Still, I crept along. I talked to Hank in the backseat the entire time, feeling like a horrible parent for taking him to such a dangerous road. I'd been an asshole for insisting on bringing him, I realized. I just hadn't known how truly awful the road would be.

We climbed higher and higher, the cliffs getting deadlier as we did. The road was just dirt for the last leg of the drive. Multiple times my car wheels spun out and struggled to keep going. I was starting to panic when I saw the last turn off. I felt like we were trapped until I saw the sign at the drive that warned about trespassers.

It was so perfectly Julian. A giant warning not to come near him matched him perfectly. I pulled into his driveway and drove up another mile of awful road that threatened to rip the bottom out from under my car. By the time I saw the big log cabin, I was so relieved that I didn't even stop to feel the butterflies that had previously been threatening to make me vomit.

I hurried out of the car and got Hank out before walking up to the front door and knocking. A growled warning came from inside, and I flinched when something smashed against the other side of the door.

"Julian? It's me, Mallory."

Silence rang out from inside the cabin, and I wondered if he was going to pretend not to be home after all the noise he'd already made. My heart pounded away in my throat and my stomach twisted. Had I come to him for no reason? What if he just didn't want me? And Hank.

"Please open the door, Julian."

A beat later, the door opened, and Julian flinched away from the light. Stepping outside, he zoned in on Hank in my arms and scowled. "What the fuck is this?"

I licked my lips and took a deep breath. I just had to stay calm and talk sense into him. "I just wanted to come talk. You left so fast the other day."

"You really dragged the kid all the way up here? Are you deranged?"

"I'm starting to wonder." I exhaled and inhaled again, breathing in some kind of liquor and cigar smoke. Wrinkling my nose, I looked behind him and noticed all the bottles set up everywhere. "Did you drink all of those?"

Looking behind him, Julian swore and shifted so his body filled my vision. "That's not your concern."

"Can I come in and talk to you?"

"No."

"Julian, please." I swallowed and started over. "I'm sorry to just show up unannounced, but I needed to speak to you. I know you're mad, but I have things I need to say and that you need to hear. So, please let me come in and talk."

He shoved his hair off of his forehead and swore. "Fine. Come in. Just don't touch anything."

I followed him into the house and looked around. The bottles were all clean and looked new. In the kitchen was a table with a single chair at it and what looked like some kind of bottling system. "What's this?"

"You're nosy, too. Great."

I got closer to one of the bottles that had a clear liquid in it and breathed in what smelled like death and destruction. "What is that?"

"Moonshine."

I frowned. "You're making moonshine?"

He just grunted as an answer.

"Is that dangerous?"

"Only if the people I sell it to act stupid."

I shook my head and turned away from the table. "Who do you sell it to? Do they act stupid often?"

Julian leaned against the kitchen counter and crossed his arms over his chest. "Is this why you came?"

I squeezed my eyes shut and shook my head. "No. This is a lot to take in, though. Where do you live? There's nowhere for you to sit or relax."

"Get to the point, Mallory."

I held Hank closer and tried to fight the urge to cry. "I just wanted to tell you that Blake and Isaac didn't know that Hank is your son. I didn't tell them. I didn't tell anyone. Not even Kara."

"What do you want, Mallory? You didn't want me in Hank's life, clearly. Why are you here now?"

"I was terrified of bringing you into Hank's life. My own parents were awful and split up when I was young. I dealt with them fighting over me when neither of them really wanted me. I was scared of making Hank's life the same. Plus, it seemed like you just wanted a one-night thing, no strings. I was wrong. I should've come back here and found you. I should've given you the option of being involved. Instead, I shut down and hid. And I'm so sorry for that.

"Then, I met Isaac, and I felt the same connection to him that I felt for you when I first saw you. And then again with Blake. I don't understand it, and it scares me, too. I care about the three of you. Too much, too fast. But it's there. I care about you."

Julian just shook his head and looked away.

"I do. I care about you a lot. Enough to back away from Blake and Isaac if you're not a part of us. I'm not going to come between the three of you. If you don't want me after what I did, I understand that. I just... I'm not willing to hurt you more than I already have. And having a relationship with Blake and Isaac like you're not missing from it would be hurtful. I want the three of you to be okay.

"And I want you to be in Hank's life." I looked around at the moonshine operation he was clearly running and winced. "I don't know this side of you. You were right when you said I don't really know you. But there are things I do know about you. That I really like. You're funny and surprisingly gentle. You make me happy."

"You want me in Hank's life? Why? Because you're just so eager to have a man like me around him?"

I moved closer to him, stopping almost immediately when he flinched away, though. "Yes. I want you in his life. And if I can say that while standing in your moonshine operation, you should really believe that I mean it."

"You have the two good brothers. Go with them and have a great life. I'm fine here."

I held Hank a little tighter. "Please, don't send me away. I want you. I know that I messed up, but I want to try again."

Turning to face me fully, Julian glared at me. "Forget it. Forget me. I hope the three of you live a happy life. He's their kid now."

I shook my head. "No. You're not listening to me. There is no us without you. If I leave this cabin without you, I'm not going back to Blake and Isaac. They can't replace you as Hank's father. It doesn't work that way. So, if you don't want us, that's fine, but we're going back to Kara's. Alone. I'm not coming between the three of you.

So, send me away if you have to, but go make it right with your brothers."

He shook his head and scrubbed his hand down his face. "You need to leave. I have some customers coming later."

Tears filled my eyes, and I nodded. "Okay. I'm sorry. This isn't how I wanted this to end."

"Yeah, well. Shit happens."

Anger and hurt whirled around in my head. "Especially when you act like an asshole."

"Go."

"I'm going." I stomped through the house and spun around to glare at him by the door. "I'm so sad for you. You're hiding from life and happiness up here in this cabin that reeks of old man, and you're too scared to take a chance on someone loving you. Even your own brothers. You let Grace win. And, having the good fortune of meeting her, that sucks. Have a great fucking meeting, Julian."

CHAPTER TWENTY-FIVE

I sat in my car for few minutes after watching Julian slam the door shut on me. Hank was buckled into his car seat, happily unaware of what'd just happened. My heart ached painfully as I forced myself to accept that things were ending. I didn't want to give up. I wanted the three of them, no matter how crazy it was.

No matter how hard I tried to stop myself from crying, it was useless. Even as I made myself turn around and start the drive down Julian's driveway, tears leaked from my eyes. I couldn't stop looking back at the cabin, hoping and waiting for Julian to run out and tell me he changed his mind. It didn't happen, though.

I pulled out of his driveway and started the horrible trip back down, all alone. The sun was starting to set and the thick tree coverage made it even darker on the road. My headlights clicked on and I drove even slower. Between wiping my eyes and nervously checking on Hank in the backseat, I wasn't as focused as I was on the drive up. My mind was all over the place, and it wasn't easy to keep going.

My phone rang from my purse next to me, and I reached over to shut it off, afraid the shrill sound would bother Hank. I looked away from the road for a split second, and when I looked back up, there was a massive deer in the middle of the road, staring into the car. I screamed and slammed on the brakes, automatically jerking the wheel to avoid crashing into the animal.

The car didn't go far since I was going so slow, but I felt the moment the front wheel slipped off the side of the road. The crunching sound of the side grating against the massive wall of rock was painful as the car came to a stop. Hank immediately started screaming, and I reached back to stroke his chest so he knew I was there.

"It's okay, baby. It's okay. Mommy made a mistake, but it's okay."

The deer continued to stare at me, unbothered. I glared at it as I put the car in reverse and gave it some gas to back up. Only, nothing happened. I gave it more gas and felt the car struggling. Still, nothing happened. I tried to open my door to look at what was happening, but the door was wedged too tightly against the side of the mountain. I rolled down my window and pulled myself out enough to see that the tire was wedged into a narrow gap between the edge of the road and the mountain. The tire was already flat, and I knew there was no way I was driving it anywhere.

Swearing and crying even more, I turned the car off and looked back at Hank. He was still screaming, even as I stretched over and took him out of his seat. Pulling him into the front with me, cradling him to my chest, we both cried together for a few minutes before I gathered myself and realized that I needed to do something. Unfortunately, I was the adult in the situation, and I needed to handle things.

Reaching over to grab my phone, I saw that the call I'd missed was from Blake. I immediately called him back and held my breath as his phone rang. I wasn't sure what to do. I'd gotten far enough down the mountain that it would be a hike back to Julian's. It wasn't like he wanted me there.

"Mallory? Where are you?" Blake's worried voice made me more emotional. Hearing someone care after feeling so rejected by Julian was too comforting.

"I'm driving down the mountain. I had a little wreck. We're okay, but the car is stuck." I cried harder when I spoke, but I couldn't stop myself.

"What'd you say? The car is stuck? Baby, we're coming, okay? Are you and Hank okay?"

"We're okay." I looked up as the deer sprinted away and heard what had scared him. The sound of loud, revving engines grew closer and louder. "I think someone's coming."

Blake swore. "It'd better be Julian."

I frowned. "It's motorcycles, I think."

"Cycles? As in plural?" Blake swore even louder. "Just hang tight, baby. We're coming to get you."

I saw the group of motorcycles come into view around the sharp turn farther down the mountain and my back stiffened on instinct. I was alone, with Hank, and I wasn't feeling safe. I didn't want to be surrounded by men that I didn't know.

"Mal?"

The men stopped several yards in front of the car and the man at the front lifted his hand in a wave. I held Hank tighter and forced a smile to what I was sure was my tear-stained and bruised face. "I'm here. They're stopping."

"Who's stopping? Men on motorcycles? How many are there?"

The leader stepped off his bike and smiled at me while pointing to my tire. He called out something, but I couldn't hear him with the windows up. "Seven. I think they're going to help with the car."

I rolled the window down enough to hear the man speaking. He was asking if they could help get my car unstuck so they could get past. Relief coursed through me, and I nodded. "Please. That would be so amazing."

"Mallory, what's happening?"

"They're going to help get the car unstuck. Oh, thank god. I just want to get off this mountain." I wiped my tears and sighed. "Julian doesn't want us."

"Ma'am? Do you have a spare in the back?"

"I have to go, Blake." I hung up, despite his protests, and looked out at the older man helping. "I do. Thank you so much for helping."

He motioned for a couple of the other guys he was with to start working on the tire. "Of course. If one of our old ladies was trapped, we'd want someone to help them, too."

I almost melted in relief. "You don't know how much this means to me."

"Not to be rude, ma'am, but you don't look like you're having the best day. The little man seems to be having some troubles, too." He smiled. "I'm Mac."

"Mallory. And this is Hank." I rubbed Hank's back and found that he was already starting to settle and yawn.

"Well, Mallory, you hang tight while we get this thing fixed for you." He patted the roof of the car. "Shouldn't be too long."

"Thank you. Really, you're a lifesaver."

I rocked Hank back to sleep and managed to get him back in his car seat, buckled in, without waking him. Mac had me start the car and put it in neutral for a minute so they could push the car out of the wedge it was in. Then, it felt like no time passed before Mac was standing next to my door and leaning down to talk to me.

"We got the spare on. You're going to need to get a new tire and rim, from the looks of it." He shook his head. "You just hit an unlucky spot."

I snorted. "You just summed up my day."

"Were you coming down from Julian's place?" Mac smiled. "Sorry to be nosy. I'd heard that J had a new woman and kid. I just figured I'd ask. We're friends of J's."

Something in the back of my brain buzzed a warning sound, but I didn't know why. I forced my smile to remain in place and shook my head. "We're not his."

"That's too bad. J's a good guy. A little steep with his prices, but I think we can get him talked down to something more to our liking." Mac's smile stretched a little too wide. "Especially with a little bargaining power."

My preservation kicked in, too little, too late. I tried to roll up the window, but Mac shoved his arm in and unlocked the door, pulling it open before I could get it locked again. I was already buckled in, so trying to scoot away from him proved fruitless. "Leave me alone!"

"Relax. No one wants to hurt a hair on your head. You fell into our lap and we're going to use you, though." Reaching over me and unbuckling my belt, he pushed at me until I climbed over the console and sat in the passenger seat. "Reba is going to drive. She's going to follow us to our place and you're not going to be an asshole about anything because of that sweet little boy sleeping in the back. Okay?"

I snarled at him. "If you touch him, I'll murder you and your mother."

Laughing, Mac reached in and roughly patted my cheek. "Damn. I think in other circumstances we really would've hit it off. I like a woman with some fire. Keep it to a low burn for now. We're not going to hurt you, and you're not going to make us. Got it?"

I shoved his hand away and moved to the backseat to be close to Hank. I couldn't stop them from taking us where they wanted to. I couldn't get Hank out and run from them. They'd catch us. If I was to take their word, they weren't going to hurt us as long as I kept my cool. I wasn't taking their word, though. "Do what you're going to do."

He laughed and motioned for a woman who'd been riding on the back of another bike to come over. "This is Reba. Be good and maybe she'll even braid your hair tonight."

"Fuck you."

"Remind me to ask J how he handles a little firecracker like you." He closed the door once Reba was settled and leaned in. "Stay close. We'll have someone behind, too."

"Got it." Reba looked through the rearview mirror at me and scowled. "You heard him. Try anything, and you'll regret it."

I glared back at her and leaned into Hank, draping myself over him. I didn't want them even looking at him. I was livid but more terrified than I'd ever been in my life. I was being kidnapped. Gently, but still. I would've fought if not for Hank. I knew you weren't supposed to let someone move you to a second location. I'd fought back against handsy men my entire life. I could definitely handle the scrawny twat in the front seat. None of it mattered, though, because I couldn't chance anything happening to Hank.

"It's okay, baby. Momma's not going to let anything happen to you." I whispered to Hank and stroked his perfect little cheeks. "We're going to have a long talk with your father when this is all over, though."

"Shut up back there." Reba, clearly high on her power trip, swerved the car enough to sling me around and get us dangerously close to driving right off the side of the mountain. "Or I'll make you shut up."

I covered Hank again, triple-checking his buckles before closing my eyes and keeping my head down. I just had to play nice and hope for the best. I wasn't great at either of those things, but I had to try. For Hank.

CHAPTER TWENTY-SIX

I was going to kill Julian. When I saw where Mac and his goons had taken Hank and me, I said a prayer that I would stay alive long enough to murder Julian and bring him back to do it again. The broken-down shed that Mac referred to as their clubhouse was very clearly a sad place where a lot of drugs were done. I could smell the cigarette smoke and despair before the door was even kicked open.

The inside was just as bad as the outside, and I immediately held Hank tighter and pulled his blanket over his head. I didn't want him breathing in the air or any of the assholes okay with kidnapping a woman and child for lower liquor prices even looking at him. I snarled at Mac when he touched my arm and pulled away.

"You're going to sit over there and play nice until I need you." He pointed to a disgusting old couch that sat way too low to the floor, like the bottom had come off. "I don't want to hear a peep from you."

I shrugged off his hold again. "What exactly do you think I'm going to be able to help you with?"

Reba appeared on my other side and dug her nails into my arm. "Move it, bitch."

"Easy, Reba. We're not going to hurt her if she behaves herself." Mac raised his eyebrows and waited until I perched on the very edge of the couch. "We're going to motivate Julian to lower his prices. To nothing. He gives us that sweet discount, and he can have you back."

I frowned. "Are you kidding? That's the grand plan?"

Mac shifted and put his hands on his waist. "What's wrong with my plan?"

"Oh, I don't know, the fact that Julian doesn't want me. He'd just turned me away when you found me. You kidnapped an unwanted woman. You're not getting shit from him for me. If anything, he might send an extra bottle of moonshine as a thank you for taking me off his hands."

"Nice try. The news is all over town about your being the Steele brothers' plaything. And that's Julian's son." Mac took a menacing step closer to me. "He may not want you, but maybe he'll care to save his son."

I sprang off the couch and glowered at him. "You're not going to touch him."

"Maybe not." Shrugging, he backed away. "Who really knows?"

"Sit back down!" Reba hissed at me, her anger nearly tangible. "You think you're so smart. You'll be sorry soon. When Julian doesn't come to rescue you and the Steele brothers move on to their next whore, you'll be ours."

A cold wave of dread and fury rolled over my body, and I did my best to sit perfectly still to avoid showing it. Blake heard me talking about men on motorcycles. Julian knew who was coming to meet him. They'd be able to find me. I just hoped they did it soon.

I tried to remain invisible as the clubhouse filled up as the night dragged on. They were having a party, preemptively celebrating getting free booze. From what I could tell, they were already getting high on something that didn't smell natural. They jeered at me when they moved past, but for the most part, no one even spoke to me. Hank was starting to get antsy and kept trying to yank the blanket off of his head, but I didn't want any part of him exposed to the things happening in the space.

I knew he was getting hungry and I knew he'd be so upset that he couldn't help crying soon. I didn't want to think about what was going to happen when we couldn't remain invisible. I was truly scared as I sat there, watching men fighting and grabbing the women around them. I could feel a few of the men staring at me. I wanted to get out of there so bad that I'd started shaking. My heart was in my throat, and I felt like I was going to throw up at any moment.

Mac came out of a back room at one point and waved his phone at me. Shouting over the music and party, he announced that moonshine was on the way. "The pretty little thing over there is to thank! Seems Julian is sweet on her after all."

I stared at my feet, sure that Julian had probably just said whatever they wanted to hear before going back to whatever he did in his cabin. He didn't care about me. Not enough, anyway.

A bottle smashed across the room, and a fight broke out between two women. The men cheered them on instead of breaking it up, and I watched in horror as blood was shed.

I had to get out of there. Everyone at the party seemed absolutely insane, and I was going to be hurt if I didn't do something. I could feel it in my bones. I wasn't safe. That meant Hank wasn't safe.

The moment I stood up, Reba was there again, shoving me down. "Get up again and I'll make sure you learn a lesson tonight."

I bit back my anger and readjusted Hank, who was starting to cry. "He needs food."

"What do you think this is, the Applebee's? He'll be fine."

"He's a baby. He needs food or he's going to start screaming his head off."

"You'd better keep him quiet," she snarled at me. "Or else."

A big man with a nasty-looking snake tattooed on the side of his face moved closer to us. "You look a little lonely, sweetheart. You want some company?"

Things were building to a fever pitch. I needed help. I had a really bad feeling in my stomach.

"Answer him!" Reba kicked my foot and hovered over me. "You think you're hot shit, but you're nothing. When someone talks to you here, you answer them with respect."

I was just opening my mouth to reply, with what, I hadn't a clue, when both doors into the building, front and back, were kicked open, and a collection of cops came running in. Chaos erupted as the drunk and drugged women and men tried to run but were taken down by eager cops. Reba was grabbed and pushed against a wall before being handcuffed, while the man who'd wanted to keep me company was pushed to his knees and threatened while another cop searched him.

The entire building was a madhouse, and I was frozen, sitting on the dirty, stained couch, feeling like I was watching a movie. Hank had started screaming, the sounds scaring him. I held him even closer and picked my feet up so a cop could hurry by to grab Mac, who was running, and throw him down.

"Move, motherfucker!" Julian's voice shook the place as he shoved past a cop and charged in. His eyes scanned the room and found me immediately. He looked like an avenging angel as he charged across the room, leaping over a chair and shoving past more cops. He saw Mac on the way, and his course changed.

I watched in horror as Julian shoved the cop off of Mac and yanked Mac off the ground. Holding him in the air by the neck, he screamed. "My woman and my kid are not your fucking bargaining tools! You're done. You're lucky I don't kill you right here, you worthless piece of human excrement!"

A cop tried to get Julian away from Mac, but Julian shrugged the cop off and threw a punch that broke Mac's nose. Mac went down, crying, but Julian grabbed him up again and threw him into a wall.

"Did you touch her? Did you fucking touch her?" He slammed his fist into Mac's stomach and then kneed him in the face when Mac doubled over.

"Baby, don't look. Don't look. Come here." Blake's voice was suddenly next to me, and I jumped as he pulled me into his chest. "We're here. Let's go."

Isaac was there, too, stroking my face and looking me over. "Did anyone touch you? Are you okay? Is Hank okay?"

I looked back at Julian and saw several cops pulling him off of Mac. He was pushed to the ground and handcuffed, his face a mask of rage as he still fought to get to Mac.

"We'll take care of him. He's okay for now. Let's just get you out of here." Isaac wrapped his arm around me and led me out of the smoke-filled building.

The moment fresh air filled my lungs, I uncovered Hank and handed him to Blake. Mind reeling, I doubled over and threw up all over a set of shiny black shoes. Wiping my mouth, I stood up and saw the shoes were attached to a scowling older man.

"Thank you for that. I was coming over to get your statement, but maybe we should wait."

"That'd be best, Detective Crane. Why don't you come to the ranch tomorrow?" Isaac pulled me into his chest and held me with shaking hands.

"Yeah, sounds good."

I looked up at Isaac and shook as my adrenaline started to wear off. "I want to go home."

Julian was brought out at that moment, handcuffed and still struggling against the three officers holding him. He saw me and instantly stopped fighting. "Red. You okay?"

I nodded through tears. "I think you need a new job."

He blinked, his own eyes wet. "Is Hank okay?"

"They would've had to kill me to get to him." I tipped my chin up, too proud to let my tears fall in front of him. I was still hearing his harsh words at the cabin. He didn't want Hank or me.

The cops pushed him forward, and he was swallowed up by the madness. I sank into Isaac's chest and groaned.

"I just want to go home," I repeated again, the same mantra I'd been chanting in my head since I'd arrived at their clubhouse. "Please."

Blake growled at someone walking by too closely and passed Hank to Isaac before scooping me into his arms. "Come on. We'll take you home. I'll have someone else drive your car home tonight."

I wrapped my arms around his neck and let him carry me to his truck. Hank's car seat was already there, and Blake put me in the back with it, knowing I'd want to be with Hank. Isaac handed me Hank, and I buckled him in before they navigated the truck past rows of cop cars and people getting arrested.

Chapter Twenty-Seven

Blake drove straight to the ranch, a stubborn look on his face. When he parked, he got out of the truck and opened the door to look in at me. "This is where you belong. With us. I need to be able to see you and touch you so I know you're okay."

I nodded, unwilling to argue, especially when I wanted to be there with them. I carried Hank inside and sank onto the couch with him. He was still fussing and tugging at my hair, but I didn't care. I was just so glad to have him somewhere safe.

"Your sister should be here any minute." Isaac sat next to me and gently took Hank from me. "You look like you're about to crumble, Mal."

"Can I take a shower?" I rubbed my eyes and rubbed at my clothes. "I just feel gross."

"Of course. You want me to sit in there with you? With Hank, so you can still see him?"

I looked over at him and felt my heart twist a little. I cupped his face and nodded. "Thank you."

Blake started the shower for me and brought me a drink while I waited for the water to warm up. Then he helped me undress and eased me under the showerhead. "Take your time. I'm going to keep an eye out for Kara."

I scrubbed my body and slowly let the tension leave my muscles. I silently cried while keeping an eye on Hank. I felt like the worse parent in the world. I'd insisted on taking him to Julian's, and I'd ended up putting him in so much danger. I felt sick.

"Out of my way! I've seen her naked before, idiot. She's my baby sister." Kara's strong voice rang through the house, and instantly, I felt a little better.

Isaac handed me a towel a second before Kara burst into the bathroom and threw herself at me. She held me tightly and cried into my hair while feeling up and down my body, checking for who knew what. When she started looking me over, even attempting to look in my armpit, I squirmed away from her and swatted at her hands.

"Kara, I'm okay." I wrapped the towel around me and let out a sigh of relief when she wrapped her arms around me and just held me. "Just shaken up. I'm really okay, though.

"I'm going to kill Julian. Then I'm going to kill every lousy piece of shit that is in that pathetic excuse of a biker club. Then I'm going to come back here and I'm going to kill you and you for not knocking sense into your brother before this." She jabbed her finger at Blake and Isaac, who looked like kicked puppies. "I can't believe you let my baby sister go up there alone. You know she survived over a decade in the city without getting kidnapped once? And she's here for less than two weeks and she gets kidnapped because she's fighting for your idiot brother! I'm going to burn this place to the ground if you don't get out of my face right now. I need a minute alone with my *baby sister*, who got kidnapped today."

Blake looked like he wanted to argue, but Isaac pushed him out of the bathroom. He came back a second later with Hank's diaper bag and handed both the bag and Hank to Kara. Then, he was gone again.

Kara looked back at me and grinned. "They're totally scared of me."

I sat on the side of the tub and reached for Hank. "I need to feed him."

"I'll do it, Mal. You need to just relax before you fall apart. I can see it all over your face." She pulled herself up on the bathroom counter and had a jar of carrots open for Hank almost like magic. Spooning it into his hungry little mouth, she looked over at me and sighed. "Today scared the shit out of me. I never want to get a call like that again."

"It scared the shit out of me, too. I've never felt so helpless. I couldn't do anything. I just sat on a couch that I'm pretty sure was made up of more sperm than fiber and waited for someone to come save us." I shook my head. "I'm buying a taser."

"I already have one on the way."

I smiled, more of the tension slipping away. "You know what's worse? I got kidnapped after being rejected. I tried to tell that idiot Mac that he was barking up the wrong tree, but he wouldn't listen. Do you know how humbling it is to have to tell a room full of people that the person they think cares about you doesn't? What a fucking slap to the face."

Kara laughed but quickly tried to hide it. "I'm sorry. It's not funny. Julian is dead when I see him."

"And a woman named Reba kept threatening me. Reba in a tube top and a visible thong." I groaned. "This whole fucking day was a bust. Honestly, I should've known when we ran into that demon at the grocery store that today wasn't my day."

"I know the exact woman you're talking about. She has an eyebrow ring that looks like it's barely hanging on to her last eyebrow hair, right?" When I nodded, Kara scowled. "She showed up at the kids' school one day last year, picking up her kid. When no one recognized her, because she hadn't been there to get her kid in the entire two years her kid had been going there, she freaked out and caused a big scene. I saw her tits twice by the time she was done."

I made a face. "Do I even want to know how?"

Giggling, Kara nodded. "When she tried to grab one of the teachers, the security guard tackled her. Boobs went flying every which way. I'm pretty sure there are still some kids in therapy over it."

"And the second time?"

Full out laughing, Kara had to put the spoon down to keep from slinging carrots all over the bathroom. "As she was storming off, she turned around and flashed everyone. I think she thought it was a moment of taking back control, but instead, she stumbled into that big tree in front of the school and I literally watched her nipple get wood burn."

I couldn't help laughing. It was what I needed. There was nothing scary about a woman who tripped with her boobs out and knocked her nipples into a tree.

"There you are. I was worried when I first saw you, but you're okay. You've always been tough." Shrugging, Kara wiped Hank's face and smiled. "I can't tell you how good it is to see you smiling. Try not to get kidnapped again, okay? You definitely took ten years off of my life tonight."

"That's not good. You're so old already."

"I should push you into that tub. How dare you."

"You'll get over it." I smiled at her and blew out the last of the tension I'd been holding. Standing up and stretching, I met my reflection in the mirror and winced. "I've never looked better."

"Nothing a few days of sleep won't fix." She stood up and kissed my forehead. "I know you'll probably say no but let me keep Hank for you tonight. You need sleep."

"I don't think I can, yet. I just need to hold him tonight."

"I figured. I brought a bag for you, too. Let me grab it." She opened the bathroom door and grunted. "The two of you need to go make her some dinner and a stiff drink. What are you doing just sitting around, eavesdropping like a couple of old biddies?"

I laughed and shook my head at her when she came back in. "Go easy on them. It's not their fault."

"Oh, I know. I'm just making sure they know they need to take extra special care of you tonight and for the next several days. Plus,

I love seeing them wince away from me." She laughed maniacally. "Makes me feel powerful."

"You're a villain; you know that?"

"I know it, and I love it." She handed me Hank and put the bag down. "Sit on the tub. I'll brush your hair like I used to."

I was so tired by the time she was done brushing and braiding my hair into the same pigtail braids she'd done on me as a kid that I could barely keep my eyes open. I pulled on pajamas and sighed. "I just want to go to bed now."

She kissed the top of my head and took Hank from me. "I brought his little travel bed. I'm going to hand him off to one of those idiots that are definitely still listening in and then go. I'll check in with you tomorrow, okay?"

I nodded and followed her out of the bathroom, happy to see the bed already turned down for me. Blake and Isaac were standing around, looking worried. I smiled as much as I could and climbed into bed. "I'm just going to close my eyes for a bit."

I barely even heard Kara threatening the guys again before I fell asleep. I didn't dream at all that night, despite the nightmare of a day I'd had. I must've been too exhausted. I didn't feel Isaac or Blake in the bed with me and I didn't hear them talking that morning, either.

The first thing I became aware of was the sun shining through Isaac's windows. I stretched and looked around for Hank, but he wasn't in his bed. My heart raced as I flew out of bed and rushed out to the main part of the house. I wasn't expecting to come face to face with Julian, but I did.

He looked me over and reached out to touch one of my braids. "Hey."

"Where's Hank?" I looked around him and saw Isaac sitting at the island, not holding Hank.

Blake popped up from the couch and held up a giggling Hank. "We're hanging out."

Relief coursed through me, and I leaned heavily against the wall beside me. I felt like I'd never be able to not worry about Hank again. He'd been threatened, and it'd activated every fear I'd ever had, plus some.

"Can we talk?" Julian moved closer to me, and I finally put together that he was really standing there.

"I thought you'd be in jail."

Isaac snorted. "Don't let him fool you into thinking he's some hardened criminal now. They didn't charge him. They just held him overnight so he'd calm down."

Julian glared at his brother. "I can handle this."

"Can you? Because you've really managed to fuck this up."

"Fuck, Isaac, I'm trying."

I cleared my throat. "I'm going to brush my teeth and wake up a bit before this starts. Can you three try not to kill each other?"

Blake grunted. "I'm just over here, being the best uncle in the world."

I bit my lip, fighting a smile. "Good job, Blake."

Chapter Twenty-Eight

I hurried through my morning routine and changed into the outfit Kara had packed for me, which ended up being a pair of leggings and an oversized t-shirt. She knew comfort. I left my braids in and then walked out to find Julian sitting on the couch, holding Hank.

My stomach fluttered and my heart slammed into my throat. Tears filled my eyes, and I froze where I was standing. It was what I wanted, and I felt hopeful seeing it. Even if Julian didn't want me, he'd still be Hank's father.

"Is this okay?" Julian came to his feet and stood there while Hank tugged at his beard.

"Of course, it's okay. You're his father."

"I was an asshole." He moved closer. "I can't tell you how sorry I am. I would be standing here for the rest of my life. Knowing that I put you in danger is something I'll never forgive myself for. You and Hank."

I was crying, but there was no hiding it. I glanced around and saw that Blake and Isaac were sitting on the front porch, giving their brother space to make things right. If he could. "I'm so mad at you, Julian. And I feel guilty for being mad at you because I hurt you first. But you were cruel to me."

He came even closer. "I fucked up. I *am* fucked up. I'm not like Blake and Isaac. They have everything together, and I just never have. Everyone sees it. I just figured you would, too."

"You're not like them, no. They're not like each other, either. The three of you are all different. And I like you each for who you are. I don't like them because they have their shit together, though, Julian. I'm not Grace."

"No, you're not. You tried to tell me that, but I wasn't listening."

"No one here wants anything from you, other than you. You should hear the way your brothers talk about you. Not today, maybe, but normal days. They care about you so much and they just want to be good with you again."

"It's embarrassing how much I feel like a failure. I never wanted to run anything, not like they did. I liked just helping them. After Grace, though, that felt like a bad thing. I needed my own thing, and I needed to be away from them. I felt like I brought them down. And I resented them for me feeling that way." He grimaced. "Look what me doing my own thing did, though.

"She's a fucking demon, and it seems like she spent a lot of energy and time breaking you down. You didn't deserve any of that. You're not a failure, Julian."

"I'm terrified of you. I have been since that first day. It never felt like that with anyone before. I thought about you almost every fucking day. For nearly two years. Then I saw you with my brothers and I just thought it was going to be the same again. Once again, I wouldn't be good enough. Only this time, it mattered even more. And then you told me about Hank."

"I'm still so sorry for keeping it from you, Julian. I was wrong."

"Well, judging by how yesterday went, maybe you should've never told me." He shook his head. "I got you both kidnapped."

I looked at Hank staring up at Julian in awe, his little face so happy, and I felt something in me slide into place. "We should start over. If you want."

He looked up at me with a hopeful smile that transformed his entire face. I'd never seen that look from him before, and I felt a part of me fall for him. "I want."

"Well, it's a little awkward because I've already given birth to your child." I grinned. "Look at me, telling you upfront."

"I always wanted to be a father." He blinked away tears and shrugged. "Kind of more than I ever wanted to be anything else."

I closed the space between us and hugged him. I just wanted to soothe his wounds and show him that he was cared for. He didn't have to fight anymore.

"Why Hank, by the way? Not that I don't love it. It's a strong name for a strong little boy."

I blushed and pulled back. "Family name?"

"Try again." He wrapped his arm around me and pulled me back into his chest. He was holding his son and the woman who wanted to be his.

I sucked in a big breath and blew it out before meeting his gaze. "When we met, there was a Hank Williams Jr. song playing. I remember thinking you had that wild look to you, and it fit the song. When I realized I was pregnant, I didn't think I'd ever see you again, but I wanted to pay homage to that moment."

"So you named him Hank."

I nodded. "I wasn't lying to you when I told you I've thought about you basically every day. I just never thought this would be a possibility."

He kissed me, lingering and breathing me in with his forehead pressed against mine. "I'm not letting you go. We're going to be a family, and we'll work through whatever comes up along the way. I'll get a different job and move to the ranch so we can all be together."

"You're definitely going to have to get another job."

"I'm sorry, Red."

"It's okay. We're okay." I looked up when I heard Blake and Isaac come in. "We're all okay."

Julian kissed me again and then looked back at his brothers. "You hear that? We're all okay."

Isaac slapped his brother's shoulder and then stroked my cheek. "I'm glad to hear it. I'm ready for things to settle down and get back to normal."

I laughed. "What the hell is normal?"

Blake looked down at his phone and groaned. "Detective Crane is coming over to get your statement."

"It's all okay. I'm feeling stronger today. And I have a lot to say about those assholes." I moved away from my men and pushed my braids behind my shoulders. "They're going to be sorry they fucked with me when I'm done with them."

Isaac cupped the back of my neck and pulled me in for a kiss. "See? Normal."

"Sorry, Isaac, there's nothing normal about this, but lucky for you, I like it." I looked around at the three of them, plus my Hank in his father's arms. "Lucky for me, you three like it."

"We're going to do dinner tonight. Kara already said she was taking Hank for the night. She's called me six times today to check on the two of you. She isn't taking no for an answer, and I'm not even going to try to tell her no. So, we're going to dinner. We're going to talk and figure out where we all stand." Blake eased me into his arms and tugged my braids. "And maybe keep these. I really could get used to them."

I grinned. "You're all terrified of my sister, aren't you?"

Julian shuddered. "She was waiting on me outside of the jail. She punched me."

My mouth fell open. "No, she didn't."

"She did. I deserved it, so it's fine."

"Oh, you poor thing." I laughed. "Did she hurt you?"

"I think you're making fun of me." Julian shook his head and gently bounced Hank. "And I think you're unaware that Blake isn't the only one who likes spanking."

A wash of heat colored my face, but I met his gaze and lifted my chin. "Oh? You both like spankings? I've never tried spanking anyone before, but I'm sure I can manage."

Isaac laughed and pulled me into him even as Blake reached for me. "Come with me, the only brother who doesn't want to be spanked."

"You think you're so funny." Blake grunted at Isaac and wagged his finger at me. "I'm going to remember this."

The sound of a door slamming outside caught my attention, and I sighed. "That was fast."

Blake immediately went into protection mode. "You sure you're up to this? I can tell him to take a fucking leap."

I smiled. "I'm up for it. Can we do it on the porch, though? I don't want to bring it in here."

"Of course." Isaac nodded at his brothers. "I'll grab you something to drink. Go on out."

Sleep and fixing things with Julian were what I needed to find my strength. I took Hank and settled into one of the rockers, facing the detective. He asked me questions, and I answered thoroughly. I didn't stop until I'd mentioned every detail of what I saw at their clubhouse, and I was assured that Mac and Reba would be in jail for a long time for the kidnapping, but also for drug charges and other warrants they already had out for their arrests.

When Detective Crane turned his attention to Julian, I grew weary. I could tell both Blake and Isaac did, too. If the man noticed the change in atmosphere, he didn't register it. "You realize that running moonshine is illegal, right?"

I sat up straighter. "There was a kidnapping in your town, Detective Crane. That's probably more important than whatever else you're looking into."

Blake growled. "And I heard that business was shut down. Not a drop left to be found."

"Never heard anything confirmed about who was running it, either. Besides what that asshole Mac was shouting off about, but you can't really trust a guy like that, can you?" Isaac's face was hard while speaking to the detective, his instinct to protect his brother strong. "So, if we could focus, that'd be great."

Detective Crane looked around at the four of us and shook his head. "I get it. I wasn't trying to start anything. I just want to be sure that it is shut down, and if what you're telling me is true, then we won't have any problems."

I smiled. "That's great."

He looked me over for a moment more and then smiled back. "Seems you boys got yourself a fighter. Good for you."

"So, everyone really does know?" I blew out a big breath. "Well, guess it is what it is."

"I think I have what I need. I'll be turning over everything to the prosecutor and she'll get in touch with you." He bid his goodbyes and left us on the porch.

Julian sank into the rocker beside me and let out a humorless laugh. "You three just went bulldog for me. Thank you."

Hank was reaching for him so hard that I had to lean forward and hand him off to Julian. "We're a...team? I honestly don't know what the hell we are, but we seem to be doing this. That means we stick together."

Blake leaned against the porch railing and locked gazes with his brother. "We're on your side. We won't let you down again, Julie."

"We love you, man."

Julian looked out at the ranch and nodded. "I love you, too."

"Now that we've resolved that, we're wanted at Kara's for Sunday brunch."

I squeezed my eyes shut. "And we're all going to that together?"

Isaac laughed. "Is there one of us you'd like to leave behind?"

"You suck. I guess we're doing this. Traveling in a pack so everyone knows I take it up the butt. I just want you all to know that I'm still pissed about no one telling me what the deal was before I fell into it. I still would've done it, probably, because I like you three idiots a lot, but I might've tried to sneak around a little more."

"Did you hear that? She likes us." Blake wagged his brows at me before wrapping his arms around my waist and tossing me over his shoulder. "Plus, the only person thinking about butt stuff is you. You pervert."

"I hate you."

CHAPTER TWENTY-NINE

We spent most of the day at Kara's and then we left to have dinner together as a...couple. I still wasn't exactly sure what to call us, but it seemed like we were committing to it. For dinner, we went to the diner and sat in a booth together, with me trying not to look like I was worried about what everyone around us was thinking.

Berna served us with a broad smile on her face. She winked at me every time I caught her eye and brought me extra ice cream with my apple pie. I found that most people who looked at us smiled at us and went about their business. It seemed like they really didn't care. By the time dessert was over and we were getting ready to leave, I was almost relaxed.

Julian was next to me, a grin on his lips as he looked down and took my hand. "Not so bad, huh?"

I bit my lip and shook my head. "I should've known you three would somehow charm the town into being cool with this."

Blake shrugged. "This is a consensual relationship between four adults who do what they want. It doesn't hurt anyone in any way. Why would they care?"

"I once had a neighbor tell me I was a bad mother because I wasn't breastfeeding Hank. Never mind the fact that I physically couldn't."

"Well, you're here now. You're ours. No one is going to treat you like that."

I grinned at Isaac even as I leaned into Julian. "Being with the three of you is so easy. I've never dated anyone and had it feel so natural."

"Isaac is right. It's because you're ours. And we're yours." Julian kissed me and then looked out the front windows of the diner. The sun was going down and it was getting darker the longer we sat there. "Now. Have we waited long enough?"

Blake nodded and slipped from the table. "I'll pay."

"Long enough for what?"

Blake leaned down and cupped my jaw. "Long enough for *our* dessert."

My stomach clenched, and I felt butterflies come to life. I knew we'd already been together, but I was nervous and excited like it was the first time. I shifted against Julian's side and actually giggled like an idiot.

Julian slid out of the booth and pulled me out with him. "Come on. I'm ready to get you home."

Isaac followed, and we all hurried to the exit as Blake paid. On the sidewalk, Isaac wrapped his arm around my shoulders and led me towards the truck. "You're dating now. Did you realize that?"

I lightly elbowed him and laughed. "I am not. I'm simply in a big situation with the three of you."

"And that situation is dating."

I was about to give my alternative argument with I looked up and found Grace coming towards us on the sidewalk. I took in her perfectly put-together outfit with her beautifully curling hair and immaculate makeup and stood a little taller. I was in pigtails, wearing a step up from pajamas, but the men around me wanted me. They didn't want that actual demon anymore.

Blake joined us on the sidewalk and pulled me in for a kiss. "Ready? Can we go? I have things I need to do to you."

I slapped his chest and nodded towards where Grace was standing, staring at us. "Maybe don't say that so loud."

Looking back, Blake saw her and nodded. "Hey, Grace."

She put her hands on her hips and looked like she was getting ready to tear into me, but Julian picked me up and threw me over his shoulder. He slapped my ass and carried me to the truck. "Bye, Grace!"

I laughed and smacked his legs. "Let me down, you neanderthal!"

Blake's slap to my ass was harder, and I knew it was him by the heaviness of it. "I'm sitting in the back this time."

Isaac swore. "I'm not driving again."

"It's your truck!" Julian put me down and jabbed at his own chest. "I always had to ride in the back growing up, and now I'm keeping that tradition. I'm in the back."

I looked around them and noticed our company was gone. "Guys, she's gone."

"Who?" Julian frowned and then kept arguing. "The back is mine. I called it."

"You didn't call it. I called it." Blake crossed his arms and put his hand over the door handle. "Isaac is driving, and you're in the front."

I raised my eyebrows and took a step back to see if they'd notice if I slipped away, but Isaac caught my arm and pulled me back. "I'm not driving."

Laughing, I looked at the three of them fighting like little boys. "You know what? No one is riding in the back with me. How about that? You three ride in the front together and I get the back all to myself."

They all went quiet and turned three adorable pouts at me. Blake shook his head. "I don't want to ride in the front."

"Too bad. All of you, get in." I frowned when they didn't move. "Or we can stand here until I'm so tired that I can barely keep my eyes open and just need to go straight to bed."

"Fine." Julian opened the front door and climbed in. "I'll ride in the front."

Once we were all inside the truck, Blake tried to pull me close to him, but I made a big show of putting on my seatbelt and resting my hands in my lap. "The three of you need to learn to play nicer together."

Julian laughed. "Who's going to teach us? You? I don't know if you learned that lesson in school, either, Red."

"I resent that." I held back a smile and twirled the end of my braid around. "Maybe I will teach you."

Blake frowned. "I'm not sure I like where this is going."

Trailing my finger down his arm, I shrugged. "None of you are going to touch me tonight until I tell you to."

Isaac stopped backing out and frowned at me. "What?"

"I'm in charge. You can all sit on your hands until I tell you to touch me." I stretched and arched my back. "Don't worry. You'll still be able to touch me. At some point."

Julian slumped in his seat and glared back at Blake. "This is your fault."

Blake grunted. "It's your fault."

I laughed into my hand and shook my head at them. They were just big kids when they were together, but there was something so sweet about it. I liked that I got both the serious and silly sides of them.

Isaac drove faster than normal, and we pulled up at the ranch while the sun was just finally setting completely. The house was dark, but I stopped Blake from turning on the lights.

"Candles. I want candles." I had an idea of how I wanted to tease them, and I needed soft lighting to be comfortable enough for it.

After they'd placed a few lit candles around the room, I walked towards the bedroom. "You three stay here. I'll be back."

There were groans as I left, but I didn't plan to keep them waiting for long. I closed myself in the bedroom and stripped down quickly before taking a fast shower. I shaved, scrubbed my body, and then dried off before pulling one of Isaac's shirts on. I heard music go on in the living room and paused at the door to gather my nerve before stepping out.

Blake was standing by the fireplace with a glass of whiskey, Isaac was sitting on the couch with his arms stretched out behind him, and Julian was perched on the edge of the chair, clearly eager for me. I smiled as I moved to the middle of the living room.

"Remember. No touching."

Blake sank onto the couch opposite Isaac and growled. "We'll see."

I bit my lip and dipped my hips to the beat of the music. "Be good, Blake."

Julian groaned. "Are you...? Yeah, you're dancing. Fuck."

I ran my hands up my thighs, catching the hem of my shirt and teasing it higher as I moved. I blushed the entire time, feeling silly until I saw their faces. They couldn't keep their eyes off of me. I moved closer to Julian and nudged his knees apart so I could stand between them and dance just for him. I bent forward and kissed him while moving my ass from side to side for my other two men.

Julian cupped my breast, but I pulled away and shook my head at him. He groaned and leaned back in his seat as I moved away to Isaac. They each groaned and reached for me while I danced for them, but I just moved away each time. Standing in the middle of them, I had them undress and sit back down, still not touching me.

I pulled my shirt up a few inches, revealing more and more of my thighs. Then, I dropped it and moved over to Julian. I straddled him and rolled my hips over him, feeling his erection trapped between our bodies. When he tried to grab my hips, I caught his arms and pinned them to the arms of the chair. I knew he was letting me hold him there, but it still made me feel sexy and powerful.

I leaned down and kissed him while I moved, stroking his lips and into his mouth to taste him. I moaned and slipped to my knees in front of him, peeling off my shirt and tossing it away before stretching forward and flicking my tongue over the head of his cock.

Julian swore loudly and grabbed for my head, but I brushed his hands away. I licked him slowly and lazily until he was lifting his hips to try to make me take more. I pressed a kiss to his tip and crawled over to Isaac. I knelt in front of him and batted my eyelashes at him while taking his cock in my hand and stroking him.

"Fuck, Mal." He grabbed for me, but I backed away, making him roughly rub his hands down his face.

Blake's hands were white-knuckled when I straddled him next. He growled when I opened my thighs wider and let his heavy erection rub against my wet lips. "Baby, you're playing with fire."

I moved off of him and then sank back on him, facing away, letting his erection get trapped between my thighs. I leaned into his chest and reached back to hold onto his neck as I grasped him with my other hand and held him steady so I could slowly sink down onto his shaft.

Julian and Isaac groaned as they got a clear view of Blake's cock disappearing inside of me. Julian gripped the base of his cock and met my eyes with a challenge. "You're about to lose your control, Red."

Blake grabbed my hips and growled into my ear. "Too fucking late."

I gasped as he easily lifted me and pounded into me from below. I realized I'd pushed them past the breaking point, but maybe that was my plan the entire time. I wanted to see how desperately they could need me. Listening to Blake swear into my ear and tell me how much he loved my body was doing magical things to me.

Blake suddenly stood up and bent me over the arm of the couch. "Let them watch you get fucked, baby. Show them how good it feels."

I gripped the couch and moaned when Blake grabbed my braids and held my head up. He thrust into me hard and fast, even while he reached around and circled my clit. I cried out his name and came hard almost instantly. Blake didn't let up, though. He slapped my ass and kept up the dizzying pace until I came again and let out a wild scream.

He pulled out and pushed into my ass, my own fluids easing his way. He swore and moaned as he went, his fingers never ceasing to circle my clit, easing the intrusion. "Jesus. Fucking hell. You were made for me, baby."

Julian moved to stand next to us, his hands finding my breasts as he kissed my neck and shoulders. "Stand up for me, Red."

I straightened with the help of Blake and moaned when Julian stepped between me and the couch. Sitting against the arm rest, he arranged himself and pulled me forward. Blake adjusted me so I straddled Julian, and they eased me down onto his cock, even with Blake's still filing me. I held onto Julian as I felt them both fill me so full, I felt like I would break. I sank my teeth in Julian's shoulder as the sensations rocked me.

Then, Julian stood up, and I was hung in the air between their cocks. I clung to them and screamed out as they took turned thrusting into me. I was lost to the pleasure as they shot me higher and higher. I didn't know if they'd been in me for a few seconds or hours, I was so far gone.

Julian swore then and shifted out of me. Blake sat back on the couch with me still on him, and Isaac pushed his cock into my core. They moved together while Julian stood on the couch next to us and offered me his cock. I opened my mouth and took him in, tasting myself on him.

My body shook as an orgasm built. Blake's arms held me from behind while Isaac filled his hands with my breasts, tweaking my nipples. Julian held my head in his hands while pushing his cock in and out of my mouth, his head bumping against the back of my throat. Feeling them all around me, consuming me, controlling me, it was nirvana. Julian reached down and rubbed my clit as he stiffened above me. It was all too big, too much. I screamed around Julian's shaft as I came hard.

Blake held me tight and growled into my ear as he came in me. He kept thrusting, kept shooting inside of me. My body convulsed and milked Isaac, forcing his orgasm from him. Julian came next, shooting his seed into my mouth. Moans filled the house as we all came together. It was loud and sweaty and so dirty as we came undone.

With their seed filling me everywhere and leaking out of me, I went limp on top of Blake and stared up at the ceiling. I felt like I'd died and gone to heaven. My nerves tingled all over, and I felt like I'd just been sunbathing on a hot summer day. I didn't even know how many orgasms I'd had, but I knew that was never going to be a problem with my mountain men. They knew how to work my body.

Julian pressed a hard kiss to my lips and sank onto the couch next to us while Isaac stumbled and sat down hard on the coffee table in front of us. I couldn't move. I just figured they'd move me if they wanted me someplace else. I was too tired, too satisfied.

Isaac swore. "This is the hottest fucking thing I've ever seen."

I looked up and saw he was staring at my core, which felt like a mess. Blushing, I patted Blake's arm to let me up and went down almost as soon as I stood up. My legs were jelly. Isaac caught me and held me in his lap, his big hands stroking the loose strands of my hair out of my face.

"You're so fucking beautiful." He pressed a kiss to my temple and smiled. "I think we're doing more than dating now."

I gave him a lazy smile. "I don't date."

Julian scoffed. "Then we'll just skip straight to the married and pregnant part."

"Pregnant?"

Blake shrugged. "Sounds good to me."

"Pregnant?" I repeated. "Are you three nuts?"

Isaac ran his hand over my belly. "It's possible, but we just know what we want. We want you."

I looked at the three of them and laughed. "You're serious."

"What'd you think we meant when we kept saying that you're ours and that this isn't over?" Blake sat up and looked me over. "Julian told us the first time you had sex you told him that you weren't his, but you were then, and you are now. You're all of ours, and we're keeping you."

I bit my lip and finally shrugged. "Okay, fine. You can keep me. I'm still not sure about the pregnant thing, though. Also, how would marriage work? And another thing, what about love?"

Julian grinned. "What about love?"

I looked at each of them and felt my chest flutter. "Love comes before marriage."

Blake pulled me back onto his lap and shared a look with his brothers. "Oh, baby. You're going to figure us out one of these days."

I laughed when Julian pulled me on top of him, all of them passing me around to shower me with love, and I looked around at them again, seeing the way they looked back at me. There was something there. Even as my heart skipped a beat, I realized what they were saying. Somehow, I'd gotten lucky enough to have gotten the love of my very own mountain men.

"Well, I think she's putting it together."

"But she doesn't date."

I laughed even as I grabbed a pillow to chuck at Isaac. Before I could throw it, I was being pulled into a heated kiss from Julian.

"She dates now."

Epilogue

One Year Later

Casey and Taylor chased after Hank as he went through the cabin, smashing whatever he could get his sticky hands on. He'd had too much birthday cake, and he was wired. He was big like his daddy, so tall for his age, and it made for a clumsy, wrecking ball of a toddler. I looked at Kara, sitting next to me with Tyler, and sighed.

"They're going to have to burn this place down when he's through in here."

Julian sank into the seat beside me and automatically pulled me into his lap. He'd recently cut his hair, and I loved the way his short hair felt under my hands. "He's fine. We were like that at his age."

I groaned as the baby kicked and glared at Isaac and Blake across the room. Something the triplets had realized not too long after I'd gotten pregnant was that I didn't get as angry about the baby pains at the man who was holding me. Somehow, it was less his fault in that moment.

Julian got to be the lucky triplet who was less in trouble in that second. I winced as something crashed in the next room of the cabin. "Blake! Isaac! Can you make sure that wasn't your child?"

Blake cut his eyes at me and shook his head. "You need an attitude adjustment, woman."

Kara laughed. "Yeah, this baby has her turning into the big, bad wolf. She punched me in the tit last week."

Isaac grunted as he passed by, on his way to find out what was being shattered. "You think that's bad? She told me that I need to trim my beard."

Julian snorted. "That *was* hurtful."

I groaned at them all and got up. "I need to pee again. Because you three put this baby in me, and now I have a bladder the size of a flea."

I heard them all joking and having fun, despite my sour mood. I was just hurting from being on my feet all day and from being seven months pregnant. My body hated me, and the baby seemed to as well. I was still having some morning sickness and my back hurt almost every single day. It wasn't a pleasant pregnancy, but I was happy. I loved my mountain men, and I even loved the cabin on top of the mountain, after it'd been renovated and the road had been repaired.

I was just cranky. My men seemed to be afraid to have sex with me the way I'd grown accustomed to. They were afraid of hurting the baby if they did too much, so they'd started insisting on not having as much sex, and having it be gentle on me. I knew it was so sweet of them, but I was craving dirty sex. I could barely focus on anything else.

We'd been at the cabin for a few days, and we hadn't had sex the entire time. With all the kids running around and company everywhere, it'd proven impossible to have even the smallest of orgasms.

I closed the bathroom door and sat on the toilet to do my business. My belly stuck out in front of me, creating a shelf that I rested the toilet paper roll on while I waited to wipe. That reminded me that I needed to have one of the guys put up the toilet paper holder. There was so much that needed done still before the baby came.

Thinking about it all made me start crying, and before I knew it, I was sobbing on the toilet when Blake walked in and leaned against the door as he locked in. He smiled as he looked me over and shook his head. "Thinking about your to do list again?"

I groaned. "I hate that you know me so well."

"What else?"

"You know what else."

"Still feeling frustrated?"

I nodded. "Turn around while I wipe."

He did and then turned back once the toilet flushed. "I talked to Isaac and Julian. They agree that you need an attitude adjustment."

I went to pull my panties up, but Blake shook his head.

"Leave them off." He moved closer. "Come here, baby."

Excitement coursed through my body as I closed the space between us. Stretching up to kiss him, I moaned as he grabbed my ass. "What kind of attitude adjustment?"

Pulling away and pushing me so that I was arched over the counter, he slapped my ass. "The kind that will help you relax some."

I braced myself on the counter and stuck my ass out for him. "Blake, I've missed you. I can handle you. You're not going to hurt me. I just need you. I need you in me."

He unzipped his pants and positioned himself at my entrance. Feeling how wet I was, he shoved into me in one hard stroke. "Stay quiet or we'll have to stop."

I was never quiet. He knew that. I was already building towards an orgasm just from having him in me, and I wasn't going to be quiet. It was impossible. Still, I nodded.

He grinned. "Hold on, baby."

I gasped as he pulled out and then thrust back in, instantly setting a fast and hard rhythm that was as punishing as it was heavenly. I cried out his name and met his heated gaze in the mirror.

He reached around and covered my mouth while driving into me even faster. We both needed it, clearly, and we both careened towards our orgasms faster than ever. He rolled my clit between the fingers of his other hand and we both came together hard, my shouted pleasure still a loud cry from around his fingers.

He held me against his chest and breathed into my hair, his hand stroking down to my belly. "You okay?"

I laughed as I caught my breath. "Are you kidding? I feel like you just exorcised whatever demon was living in me."

He grinned and turned me around to hold me properly. "I'm sorry we weren't listening to you before. This is the first pregnancy we'd been involved with and we're terrified of hurting you."

I looped my arms around his neck and smiled up at him. "I know. I love you for how much you care about me, but I'm still a woman. I still have needs."

"Oh, we know you're a woman, baby. I don't know how many times I've had to take care of myself lately. Seeing you like this, pregnant with our baby, it makes me want to fuck you long and hard, all day long." He kissed me gently. "But your health comes first."

"What made you three decide to change your mind today?" I grinned. "And how'd you get the privilege?"

"We talked to Kara about it. Which I know is weird, but she knows shit." He shook his head. "She told us that we needed to rail you before she had to put a muzzle on you."

I threw my head back and laughed, knowing those were the exact words my sister had used. "Lovely."

"And I won because Isaac is chasing Hank and Julian got roped into a conversation with Tyler. I was rude enough to walk away from it."

"Bless your rudeness."

"I love you, baby. I just want to take care of you. You know that."

I did. And I could see it and feel it after my orgasm. I hugged him and sighed into his chest. "I feel so much better."

"You want to go back out and play nice with your sister? Isn't that something you said to me before?"

"I'll still kick your knees out from under you, Blake Steele. Don't forget that."

"Never. You make sure of that, Mallory Steele."

I grinned at hearing the name, suddenly all sunshine and rainbows. I might've even skipped while joining everyone in the kitchen again. I looked around and saw Hank with a marker, coloring his face blue, Casey and Taylor fighting over Kara's phone, and then watched as my men started fighting amongst themselves.

I sank into my seat, feeling the soreness that only came after really fantastic sex, and watched as Blake, Isaac, and Julian fought with the same silent intensity as Casey and Taylor. I knew they were fighting over Blake sneaking away with me. I could tell by the way they ribbed him and he puffed his chest out at them. I giggled and looked over at Kara.

She and Tyler were watching me with smirks on their faces. "Well, it seems that all you needed to slip away into euphoria was an orgasm."

I grinned and nodded, all peace and flowers. I was still tingling from it as I watched Casey take Taylor in a headlock just as Julian did the same to Blake. The five of them fumbled around the kitchen, knocking over a plate of lasagna and sending spaghetti sauce everywhere. Hank went straight to the mess and flung himself in it. Still, I smiled.

Kara looked from me to Blake and then to Tyler. "You know what? We're going to go see if we can't find some of what you had. Just let the guys parent the kids for a while."

Tyler, healed and healthy, stood up and threw Kara over his shoulder. "This is awesome!"

I waved them off and laughed when Isaac slipped in the mess and dragged his brothers down with him. The house was destroyed, Hank was a mess, and all the siblings were battling it out with food fights, but I didn't care. I was happy. I had my men, the ones I'd married in a union service, and I had my happy home. Things were good.

"He's giving me a wedgie! Make him stop!"

I wasn't even sure what set of siblings that plea for help had come from. I just kicked my feet up at the table and breathed out a happy sigh. Things were so good.

"Don't lick me! What are you, five?"

Again, not sure who that'd come from. I picked up the paper from the table and flipped to the comics. I especially related to Denis the Menace those days, but at that moment, I didn't identify with the old guy as much as normal.

"Hey! Stop biting!"

I looked over the paper and saw Julian with his mouth on Blake's leg as Blake held Julian in some kind of headlock with his thighs. Isaac was wrapped around Blake, and Casey and Taylor were next to them, rolling around in lasagna as they fought. I could've stopped it. They wrestled so often that I'd perfected the art of crying out in pain to distract them, but I didn't feel like it. I was relaxed from head to toe, so I just lifted the paper back up and kept reading the funnies.

"Who the hell farted?"

Still wasn't my problem.

I hope you loved reading Mountain Men Triplets!
If you want more hot triplet brothers for keeps check out my debut reverse harem novel:

My Best Friend's Triplet Brothers

for $2.99 or FREE in Kindle Unlimited

FREE PREVIEW OF MY BEST FRIEND'S TRIPLET BROTHERS

If I'd known that I'd have Warren Strickland's face between my thighs in less than two hours, I would've been slightly more uncomfortable. As it was, I was able to face Macy, my best friend, without wanting to run and hide.

Macy, dressed in a pretty white sundress, took a long pull from her cocktail and leaned into me. "Can you believe it's finally happening?"

I squeezed her arm and smiled. "I'm so happy for you, Mace. You deserve this."

She rolled her eyes. "I'm not sure anyone deserves the monstrosity that is this wedding, but I'll take it."

"You deserve it. It could be even bigger and you'd still deserve it."

"Even bigger than a two-week-long event planned by my neurotic wedding planner and paid for by my neurotic brother? You do realize that there's a dance planned, right? A full-on fucking dance. And a karaoke night. I'm not sure I was thinking clearly when I signed on for all of this."

I laughed. "Mace, the dance was your idea!"

"You're right. It's all starting to feel a bit much now. People don't do this. People don't have weddings like this. Who do I think I am?"

Leaning into her, I squeezed her face in my hands lovingly. "You're Macy Strickland. You're amazing, and you're having the wedding you deserve. End of story."

"You're right. That it's the end of the story, anyway." She turned to face me fully and caught my hand in hers. "I'm so sorry about Milo."

My stomach tightened and I fought to keep the scowl off my face. Letting go of her, I leaned back in my seat. "Screw Milo."

"I agree. Screw Milo. He was a jerk, anyway."

I laughed. "You loved Milo."

Draining her glass, she waved me away like I was an annoying mosquito. "I wouldn't say loved. He was just an improvement over the last asshole you were with. At least, I thought he was. Turns out, he was the same asshole in a different package."

"A smaller package." I snorted.

"No!" she gasped dramatically and then groaned. "You never said anything about it!"

I took a long drink of my margarita and shrugged. "What was I supposed to say? The man I think I love has a mediocre penis, at best?"

"Did he at least know how to use it?"

I cast a long look at her and then rolled my eyes. "Why do you think I've been so tense for the past two years?"

"Oh, Sara. I'm so sorry. You deserve so much better. You deserve this." She gestured around at the stunning resort we were sitting in. "It's not fair that you always attract the losers."

I winced. "We can't all attract angels."

Macy pouted and wrapped her arms around my shoulders in a tight hug. "I'm sorry. That was rude of me. It's not your fault. Men just suck. All men except Jason."

That same tightening in my stomach grew worse with hearing her voice the same thing I'd been thinking. Her fiancé was amazing. Jason was kind, handsome, funny, and he'd literally give his life to make Macy happy. I couldn't find a man who'd give up other women for me.

"Oh, Sara! I made you sad! Come on, let me cheer you up. The pool is amazing. Let's go swimming." She pushed away from the bar. "Or there's the sauna. We can sweat out the bad energy."

I pulled my best friend into a tight hug and shook my head. "I love you. I'm fine. I think I'm going to take a nap before the barbeque tonight. It was a long flight and I'm exhausted."

"You promise you're okay?"

I smiled but remained silent. I didn't want to lie to her. I knew I'd be okay, but I was filled with so much anger and hurt at Milo that I just wanted to scream. I hadn't gotten the angry confrontation out of my system when I'd found out that Milo was a cheating asshole. I'd just left and hadn't looked back. No matter what, though, Milo wasn't going to break me.

"Fine, fine. Just take your nap. I'll make sure that we cheer you up tonight. I'm sure seeing the entire family will just bring the biggest smile to your face."

I didn't miss her sarcasm. I let out a frustrated little groan and dropped my head back. "I might sleep through it."

"No, ma'am. You have to be by my side. I'll be there to protect you from my big, bad brothers." She laughed. "It's not like when we were kids, though, Sara. They've grown up some."

I knew they had. I'd just seen an article on Andrew while flipping through a magazine the week before. He was edging his way towards becoming a billionaire and the journalist had captured his stern stare in the photograph they'd printed. It should've been a sin how beautiful the triplets were. Too bad they were demons.

"Oh, come on, Sara. Things are different now. How long has it been since you've actually spent any time with them?"

"About ten years, by choice." I shuddered at the memories and backed away. "I'll be there tonight, of course. I'll be the one with bells on, happy for you."

"Don't be late! You know my cousin, Maggie, is here. She'll be glued to my side if you're not there."

"So, you only want me to be there as a block against your family? I see how it is." Smiling, I waved goodbye to her and strode towards the front desk.

I hadn't bothered to check in before meeting Macy at the bar. Despite my personal problems and my funky mood, I was so happy for her. I was eager to spend the next two weeks prepping for the wedding with her and just being with my best friend. We'd been busy in our own lives lately, and I hadn't seen her enough.

The front desk receptionist greeted me warmly and tapped away at her computer for a moment. She was just about done with me when the phone rang and she had to answer it. I was daydreaming about the bed that I knew would be super fluffy when she gasped and dropped the phone.

"I have to go. My cat is sick." Tears filled her eyes, and she backed away. "Oh, my god. I have to go."

She fled from the front of the resort, leaving me standing there, staring after her in shock. I felt terrible for her, and terrible for just standing and watching her, but I was also a little shell-shocked.

It took a minute for someone else to help me, and when they did, they seemed as flustered as I was. The older man apologized profusely, despite me telling him that I was fine. I even went as far as explaining that the woman's cat was sick in hopes of her not getting in trouble. Still horrified, the man quickly handed me a key card and a certificate for a free massage while I was at the resort.

I would've spent more time trying to defend the woman and soothe the man's worries, but he seemed so eager to get rid of me that I just grabbed my bag and headed towards my room. Before running away, the woman had mentioned I was to go down the grand stairs and towards the right, but looking at the room number on my key card, I needed to go left.

I took my time moving through the resort, looking around. The grand ceilings, the tall walls of natural stone, the sweeping wood floors, it was all so stunning. Set against the massive picture of nature that showed through the big windows, the whole resort felt warm and comforting. It was a modern cabin that I never would've been able to afford if the entire event wasn't being paid for by Andrew.

I felt small walking through the huge, window-lined hallway that led to the rooms. Everything was so pretty, and the snow on the ground outside made me feel like I was in a winter wonderland. Macy was a very lucky bride. She was going to have the most beautiful wedding, at the most beautiful resort. It was impossible not to feel the smallest smidge of jealousy, but I really was so happy for her. She'd gone through her own fair share of frogs to find her prince charming and she deserved her happy ever after.

Still. It would be nice to find my own. Instead, I just kept stumbling upon more and more frogs. With warts. Metaphoric warts.

Finding my room, I stared at the plaque on the double doors in confusion. It read Marigold Suite. I didn't think I'd gotten a suite. With Andrew paying for everything, I was surprised that I'd gotten anything at all. I half expected my key card to not work as I swiped it, but it did.

Feeling a bud of excitement blossom in my chest, I hoped that things were taking a turn for the better for me. I could hope. It was fine to hope.

Pushing into the suite, I looked around in awe. More of the cathedral ceilings stretched into the entrance, with beautiful hardwood under my feet. Plush rugs led farther into the suite. I could see a massive fireplace glowing with a real fire on the other side of the room, next to a wall of windows that looked out over the tundra behind the resort.

Excitement had me rushing into the back part of the suite, the bedroom. A massive bed looked welcoming, and I couldn't help but jump on it. Staring up at the ceiling, I breathed out a sigh of relief. Things were going to be okay. Based solely on the comfort of the bed under me, I knew things were going to be okay.

I stood up to look around the rest of the suite and realized that I could hear a shower running from one of the other rooms nearby. How strange. I wouldn't think that sound would carry so easily in such a nice resort. I walked towards the sound, wondering how quiet I was going to have to be during my stay. I didn't want to bother anyone staying on either side of me.

A door off the other side of the bed, as tall as two of me, seemed to be the source of the sound. Instantly worried, I slowly crept towards it and grabbed the big handle. Pressing my ear to the door, I frowned as a low grunt filled my senses. Without another thought, I pushed open the door, expecting to see a closet that shared a wall with the adjoining suite. Instead, I found myself standing in a bathroom, across the room from Warren Strickland.

Warren Strickland, standing in a steamy shower, one arm braced on the wall, one big hand wrapped around his equally big cock. Fist pumping, he jacked himself off with a slow intensity that instantly flooded my panties with desire. Too much man, too much testosterone—too much cock.

I gasped and turned my back, something that was harder than it should've been. "What are you doing?"

The water turned off, and a low growl filled the bathroom. "What am *I* doing? What are *you* doing?"

I peeked back at him and squeaked when I found him still naked, still standing with his cock in his hand. "Oh, my god. What are you doing?"

"You already asked that." He growled the words out. "I think it's pretty fucking obvious what I'm doing. Now do you mind telling me why you're in my bathroom?"

"*Your* bathroom? This is my bathroom!"

"Sorry, Cupcake, but this is *my* bathroom. My bathroom and my room. How'd you get in?"

I felt my face go blood red. Was I in his room? How would that be possible? "A key. I got a key from the front desk. It had this room number on it."

"Someone fucked up."

I braced myself against the door and nodded. "Seems that way."

"I'm getting over the shock." Warren's smooth voice sounded from right behind me. "And I'm not all that mad about it."

A shiver went down my spine at the feeling of his body heat so close to me. Stepping back into the room, I hurried to the end of the bed, where my purse was, and glanced back at him. Still naked. "There was a woman with a cat, and I guess that's what happened. I'll go."

"A cat?"

I cast one last long look at the view from the suite and shook my head. "Never mind. I'm going. This was not how I planned on starting this trip. I'm so sorry to interrupt."

I groaned to myself when I realized I'd just apologized for interrupting his jacking off. I couldn't get out of there fast enough. I grabbed my purse and tried backing away without looking back at Warren. It wasn't easy. He was beautiful. They'd always been beautiful, though. There'd always been something about them that made my blood heat up just a little bit too much.

"It's good to see you, Cupcake. You look good."

I frowned. "Thanks. Good to see you, too, I guess."

"You don't have to leave."

My head snapped around to face him before I could think twice. "What?"

His crooked grin was so damn charming. It always had been. It was the defining thing about him that made it so clear that he was Warren and not his brothers. "Stay."

A tingle went through my body as I stared into his face. He was older; his face was broader and stronger. There was a shadow of a beard across it, and those bright blue eyes weren't as mean as I remembered them in my head. They were softer, sensual with thick black lashes that I could practically feel brushing across my skin. I repeated that same one-word question. "What?"

Warren smiled. "Stay, Cupcake....."

Continue Reading My Best Friend's Triplet Brothers

for $2.99 or FREE with Kindle Unlimited

Printed in Great Britain
by Amazon